CHURCHILL

A BEGINNER'S GUIDE

CHURCHILL

A BEGINNER'S GUIDE

NIGEL RODGERS

Hodder & Stoughton

A MEMBER OF THE HODDER HEADLINE GROUP

Orders: please contact Bookpoint Ltd, 130 Milton Park, Abingdon, Oxon OX14 4SB. Telephone: (44) 01235 827720, Fax: (44) 01235 400454. Lines are open from 9.00–6.00, Monday to Saturday, with a 24-hour message answering service. Email address: orders@bookpoint.co.uk

British Library Cataloguing in Publication Data
A catalogue record for this title is available from The British Library

ISBN 0 340 80426 2

First published 2001
Impression number 10 9 8 7 6 5 4 3 2 1
Year 2007 2006 2005 2004 2003 2002 2001

Cover photo by Bettman/Corbis
Typeset by Transet Limited, Coventry, England.
Printed in Great Britain for Hodder & Stoughton Educational, a division of Hodder Headline Plc, 338 Euston Road, London NW1 3BH by Cox & Wyman, Reading, Berks.

CONTENTS

1 Churchill – Childhood and Youth

Statesman, soldier, writer, painter, Churchill is one of the twentieth-century's key figures. The most far-sighted and determined opponent of Hitler, he was famed for his large cigars, eccentric hats, defiant V-for-Victory signs and heroic wartime speeches. In World War II he almost literally embodied the spirit of British resistance to Nazi Germany. But Churchill's political career had begun 40 years before he became Prime Minister in 1940. By then he had already held most of the high ministerial posts, some when he was very young. Both his life and career were markedly irregular, for he was frequently out of office, once for a whole decade, and he changed sides not once but twice. Initially a Conservative MP, he abandoned the Tory party after only six years to become a Liberal, finally returning to it after many vicissitudes. Anyone can rat, he said later, it takes genius to re-rat. If he was a statesmen of noble descent, the last aristocrat 'to rule – not just preside, rule – over this country', in C. P. Snow's words, he was also a maverick, sometimes a rebel, and one with an impish sense of humour. Part of his rebelliousness he may have inherited from his impetuous, even rash parents; part came from his own almost frantic determination to succeed.

Winston Spencer Churchill was born on 30 November 1874 at Blenheim Palace, Oxfordshire, the home of his grandfather, the seventh Duke of Marlborough. With its towers, arches and immense park, Blenheim is one of Britain's grandest if least habitable houses. It was built for John Churchill (1650–1722), the first Duke of Marlborough and brilliantly successful commander of Britain's armies against Louis XIV's France, and a direct ancestor of Churchill. Blenheim's flamboyant architecture and romantic parkland made a suitable birthplace for a man who never easily accepted the restraints of British political life but who held deeply romantic views of his country and its destiny.

Churchill was born at Blenheim, he proposed to his wife at Blenheim and within sight of Blenheim he lies buried, in Bladon churchyard.

His father, Lord Randolph Churchill, was born in 1849, the younger son of the Duke of Marlborough. His mother Jennie was born in 1854, daughter of a New York financier, Leonard Jerome. Jerome was later American consul in Trieste where Jennie spent her first years. The next few were spent in Paris, amid the most glittering circles, and then in the summer of 1873 the Jeromes visited England. At a ball on a yacht belonging to the Tsarevich, the heir to the Russian throne, Jennie met Lord Randolph. Within three days they were engaged, despite the disapproval both of the snobbish Duke and of Mr Jerome, who had his doubts about Lord Randolph. But the young people were determined and in April 1874 they were married. The same month Lord Randolph was elected to Parliament for the local constituency of Woodstock. (Being a duke's younger son, he did not sit in the House of Lords.) The couple now rented a house in London where they entertained lavishly, the Prince of Wales, later Edward VII, being among their guests. Only seven and half a months later Winston, their first son, was born at Blenheim – apparently prematurely, after Jennie had had a riding accident in the park. Symbolically, Lord Randolph was away at the time.

Churchill was at first a frail baby, but he soon gained weight and health. His improvement, however, owed little to his mother. Jennie Churchill, now at her zenith as one of the great society beauties of the age, was preoccupied with entertaining. Churchill adored her but saw little of her. 'She shone for me like the evening star. I loved her dearly – but at a distance', he said later. Instead, he turned for affection to his nanny, Mrs Elizabeth Everest, a devout and kindly woman whom he called 'Woomani' and to whom he opened his heart, writing to her from school and later from the army. When she died in 1895, Churchill was at her bedside, calling her 'my dearest and most intimate friend'. Such maternal absence in childhood was common among the British upper classes at the time, and Jennie did not entirely neglect her son. She arranged for a governess to give him his first lessons – including maths, which he detested – and appeared intermittently to dazzle or reprove him. He was generally considered a 'troublesome' child – his dancing teacher thought him the naughtiest boy in the world – but docility was never a Churchillian trait.

At the age of seven, Churchill was sent to his first boarding school in Ascot – again, normal upper-class practice. Unfortunately the school, though well-equipped – it even had electric lights, then a novelty – was run by a sadistic clergyman who flogged the boys until they bled. Churchill stoically did not complain but one holiday Mrs Everest saw his scars and told his mother. He was swiftly moved to a school in Brighton run by two spinsters, where he was much happier despite a bad attack of pneumonia. Dancing, riding and swimming supplemented the core subjects of Maths, Latin and Greek. Churchill did not shine at the latter two but did better at English and History, coming top of the school by the time he left at the age of 13. In 1888 he went on to Harrow School (chosen because of its supposedly healthily elevated position) despite fainting from anxiety during the Latin paper in the entrance exam. He had no real need to worry, for the headmaster was happy to take the son of such a famous politician as Lord Randolph.

Churchill had seen even less of his father than of his mother during his childhood. A visitor recalled Lord Randolph at breakfast briefly acknowledging the presence of his two sons before returning to reading his newspaper. But he had an excuse, which Churchill himself eagerly accepted: his political career had taken off dramatically in the 1880s. Although at first preferring a glamorous London social life to making a career in Parliament, Lord Randolph had found himself ostracized after quarrelling with the Prince of Wales in a divorce scandal. He turned his considerable if erratic energies to studying social problems, formulating a radical doctrine of his own called 'Tory Democracy' – then considered something of a contradiction in terms, for the Tories distrusted democracy generally. Instantly recognizable due to his long moustaches and bulbous eyes, Lord Randolph proved a brilliant orator, ridiculing both the Liberal Prime Minister William Gladstone and some fellow Conservatives for their feebleness. He travelled the country making rousing, even risqué public speeches which earned him the nickname 'Cheeky Randy' and which appealed to those working men who had recently won the right to vote in the 1867 Reform Bill. In the Commons he urged the Conservatives to continue the reformist policies of Disraeli, their great leader who died in 1881. With some other Tory Democrats, he formed the so-called 'Fourth Party', wittily harassing both sides until he was made Secretary of State for India in 1885 in a new Conservative administration. He proved an able if impetuous minister, ordering the strengthening of the Indian army and the annexation of Upper Burma. In 1886 he became Chancellor of the Exchequer and Leader of the Conservatives in the House of Commons (Lord Salisbury, the Prime Minister, was in the Lords), remarkable achievements for a man aged only 37. Unfortunately, he clashed with the rest of the Cabinet over his very first budget in 1887 for trying to reduce spending on the navy. When Salisbury rejected his proposals, he rashly offered to resign, thinking himself indispensable. He was not, for Salisbury accepted his offer and he had to retire to the backbenches. His political career was effectively over before he was 40.

Lord Randolph might have managed to return to office later but not very long afterwards the first signs of illness began to cloud his mind and affect his speeches in the Commons. It was syphilis, then incurable and almost unmentionable. Churchill, who had followed his father's brilliant career with intense pride, going to the House of Commons to hear him speak, was at first unaware of this, for he saw no more of him while he was at Harrow than earlier. At Harrow, Churchill was neither brilliant nor a dunce, despite his later comments about his academic failings. He won a school prize for reciting all 1,200 lines of Macaulay's *Lays of Ancient Rome*, an early indication of his prodigious memory which he would later put to good use, and again showed promise in English and History. But in the vital subjects of Latin and Maths he lacked concentration. Socially he seems to have been a distinct loner, with few friends. His mother was still notably absent even on his holidays, and seldom visited him at school. 'Please do, do, do, do, do come down to see me … I have been disappointed so many times about your coming', he wrote to her at the age of 16. His far more conventional younger brother John, who later became a stockbroker, was a poor substitute, although he took part in Churchill's elaborate war games at home.

Physically the adolescent Churchill, with reddish hair and rounded features, was puny and frail-looking, and small for his age. In one significant incident he hid behind a tree when some other boys threw cricket balls at him. Ashamed at his cowardice, he resolved in future always to seek out, rather than avoid, physical danger. This tendency seems to have become second nature to him, and he often alarmed later companions with his boyish love of 'bangs', as he called gunfire. At the age of 18, when on holiday at Bournemouth, this new determination led to his jumping off a bridge to avoid being caught in a game. He calculated, wrongly, that a tree would support him and fell 30 feet. He ruptured a kidney, was unconscious for three days and convalescent for three months. But the accident did not affect his verve. At Harrow he also developed a keen interest in fencing, winning a silver medal in the Public Schools Competition due 'to his quick and dashing action, which quite took his opponents by surprise'. At the age of 17 he spent a few months in France, developing a deep affection for the country and an idiosyncratic if powerful way of speaking French. His father, unimpressed by his son's school record, finally decided that he should go not to university but into the army via Sandhurst, a normal career for the less academically gifted.

Churchill in fact failed the Sandhurst entrance exam twice and had to go to a 'crammer', finally scraping through in the summer of 1893. Although life at Sandhurst was demanding – cadets rose at 6.30 a.m. for a strenuous day spent riding, learning musketry, digging trenches, reading maps – Churchill took to it, becoming a particularly good horseman. 'No hour is lost that is spent in the saddle', he declared. His father, although disgruntled by Churchill's expenses – the cavalry which he had chosen was the most expensive branch of the army – soon found him 'much smartened up', and took him with him on a visit to his friend's (Lord Rothschild) house at Tring. There for the first time they discussed politics over cigars. Sadly, the budding father and son relationship, for which Churchill had long hoped, was curtailed by Lord Randolph's rapidly worsening health. Accompanied by Lady Jennie, Lord Randolph set out on a world cruise to try to improve his health but when he returned in December 1894 he was mortally ill. He died in January 1895 and was buried at Bladon, near Blenheim. 'All my dreams of comradeship with him, of entering Parliament at his side and in his support, were ended. There remained for me only to pursue his aims and vindicate his memory,' Churchill wrote later.

That year, 1895, the death of his old nanny Mrs Everest cut another tie to the past. Suddenly, Churchill had to grow up fast. He now became head of the family, one facing acute financial problems. Despite some successful speculations in South Africa, his father had squandered much of his own inheritance. His irresponsibly extravagant mother had within three years of his father's death amassed debts of £14,000. (The pound was then worth perhaps 50 times as much as today.) Churchill 'passed out' of (graduated from) Sandhurst 20th out of 130 cadets – a big improvement on his school days – and joined the Fourth Hussars, but this was a 'smart' and expensive regiment. His officer's pay of £120 per year did not begin to cover expenses on drink, horses and clothes incurred in keeping up with his fellow officers. These came to about £500 more. A polo pony costing £100, for example, was obviously indispensable to him – but so was a new ball gown costing £200 to his mother. Clearly, he would have to succeed dramatically, inside or outside the army, just to pay the Churchill family debts. But he was almost recklessly ambitious anyway.

Soldier and Reporter 2

Churchill joined the Fourth Hussars, a cavalry regiment based at Aldershot, Surrey, in February 1895. He was longing for military action in which he could shine and worried this could be hard to find in such peaceful times. A man who had actually fought had, he felt, an 'an aura about him'. Convinced that, like his father's, his life would be short, he felt he had no time to waste. At first, however, like every other new officer, he underwent six months of rigorous training in the saddle. He also played polo frequently, at which he excelled.

If relatively poor (for an aristocrat), Churchill had excellent connections thanks both to his father's past political career and to his mother. Jennie Churchill reputedly had numerous lovers; she certainly had many influential friends, to whom she wrote begging letters on her son's behalf. In his early career Churchill exploited these contacts ruthlessly. He was chosen to escort the Duke of Cambridge, the army's elderly Commander-in-Chief, during an official visit to Aldershot when he also met the Prince of Wales and the Duke and Duchess of York, later King George V and Queen Mary. He was invited to a ball almost every night, although he was often too tired to go. In October, he finally found a war he could join – in far-off Cuba, which had revolted against Spain. He made use of the army's generous leave to travel and of Lord Randolph's old friendship with Sir Henry Drummond-Wolff, then ambassador to Madrid, to obtain an introduction to Marshall Campos, the Spanish commander. With a subaltern friend, he sailed via New York, arriving in Cuba in late November 1895. Although officially only observers, the two young Englishmen joined a column of Spanish troops in action. On 30 November, his twenty-first birthday, Churchill had his 'baptism of fire' when guerrillas fired on the column while he was having breakfast. A bullet passed within inches of him, killing the horse behind him.

Churchill described his adventures in five 'letters' for the *Daily Graphic*, for which he received £5 a piece. So started his combined career as reporter and soldier – an irregularity that offended many in the army. After only three days in the war zone, he returned home with a newly acquired taste for Cuban cigars and for the siesta, a lifelong custom that later helped him to stay up half the night working.

Back in England, he began scheming to reach other war zones such as Crete, in revolt against the Ottoman Turks, or Matabeland (now Zimbabwe). 'A few months in South Africa would earn me the South Africa medal', he explained to his mother. 'You really ought to leave no stone unturned to help me.' But in vain. Instead, he resumed a Hussar subaltern's busy social round, going to balls, country house parties and dinners. When in 1896 the Fourth Hussars were posted to Bangalore – in southern India, far from any possible fighting – he thought of resigning his commission, but instead sailed with a heavy heart. Disembarking from his ship, he wrenched his right shoulder – an injury that weakened his right arm for life. He could never again play tennis, and played polo only with his right arm strapped up. He also began using a Mauser pistol rather than a sabre when mounted.

Life in Bangalore was comfortable and relaxing, as Churchill remarked: 'If you liked to be waited on... all you had to do was to hand over all your uniform and clothes to the dressing boy, your ponies to the syce [groom] and money to the butler and you need never trouble anymore.' But idleness did not suit him and he busied himself in self-education, reading Gibbon's *Decline and Fall of the Roman Empire* and Macaulay's *History of England*. Their majestic, long-winded prose was to influence his own resonant style. He also read Plato, Darwin, the pessimistic philosopher Schopenhauer and a biography of Napoleon, a lifelong hero. But generally he found British-Indian life dull. On leave in England in spring 1897, he made his first political speech (as a Conservative) in Bath, and was relieved to find that his audience did not seem to notice his lisp – he could never pronounce 's' properly.

In April 1897, news of fighting on India's mountainous north-west frontier (now the Afghan/Pakistani frontier) led Churchill to approach General Sir Bindon Blood, commander of the Field Force being formed to crush a revolt by the Pathans. General Blood, whom he had met, let Churchill accompany the force as war correspondent for the *Daily Telegraph* and the Calcutta Pioneer. Churchill hurried back to Bangalore, gained his regiment's permission and hurried again 2,000 miles north for his first real fighting. This proved nasty, not glorious, warfare. The Pathans fought back with furious bravery against the British columns advancing to burn their villages, part of a scorched earth policy which Churchill admitted was 'cruel and barbarous'. Both sides used dumdum bullets – soft-nosed bullets which make vicious wounds and were later banned internationally – and there were many casualties. Due to these, Churchill soon joined the force as an active soldier, galloping around and exposing himself unnecessarily to danger to win fame. 'I rode on my grey pony all along the skirmish line where everyone else was lying down in cover. Foolish perhaps but... given an audience, there is no act too daring or too noble', he wrote revealingly to his mother. On 16 September, his column, on its way back to base, was attacked by Pathans and out of 1,300 men, 150 were killed or captured. Churchill, commanding the rearguard at one stage, thought he had shot four Pathans and was mentioned favourably in General Blood's despatches (report), to his delight. But, to his chagrin, in October he had to rejoin his regiment in Bangalore.

He described his experiences in *The Story of the Malakand Field Force*, his first book written at breakneck speed and published in the spring of 1898. Despite many typographical errors, which made him 'scream with disappointment' – the fault of an uncle who volunteered to correct the proofs – the book was well received. *The Times* admired his 'power of direct expression ... and sense of humour'; the *Spectator* thought he showed 'keen powers of soldierly observation'. Lord Salisbury, the Prime Minister, read the book admiringly, and Churchill earned two years' pay in royalties. But some officers deplored his criticism of official policies, such as the 'forward policy' on the frontier, thinking him pushy and presumptuous. That spring in Bangalore Churchill wrote his only novel, *Savrola.* It relates how a tyrannical government is overthrown by Savrola, a courageous, intelligent, well-read young hero, who 'appreciated all earthly pleasures ... who hoped for immortality but contemplated annihilation with composure' – in fact, very like the young Churchill. The book was first serialized in Macmillan's Magazine for £100. When it appeared as a book, it had mixed reviews; the Manchester Guardian said it had 'cheery vigour', but the Globe saw it as 'only too obviously the work of an amateur'. It recalls rather closely Anthony Hope's recently published *Prisoner of Zenda* and Churchill perhaps had reservations about it. Anyway, his attention soon returned to military matters.

In 1898, the British decided to reconquer the Sudan, formerly an Anglo-Egyptian province but ruled by the Mahdi (Dervish messiah) since General Gordon had been killed at Khartoum in 1885. Churchill, again on leave in England, was desperate to join the army commanded by Kitchener but Kitchener, despite Jennie Churchill's letters, was prejudiced against a man whom many now saw as a 'medal-hunter'. Finally, thanks to Lord Salisbury, Churchill was attached to the 21st Lancers, another cavalry regiment, and the *Morning Post* agreed to pay him £15 a piece for reporting the war.

In early August, after riding two horses to death and getting lost in the desert overnight, he finally caught up with the Lancers and the Anglo-Egyptian army advancing south in blinding heat. He was in time to take part in the Battle of Omdurman on 2 September 1898, when Kitchener's army faced the Dervishes outside Khartoum. The Dervishes' superior numbers counted for nothing against the fire power of massed Lee-Enfield rifles and Maxim machine guns. The cavalry played little part until Kitchener ordered an advance against the retreating Dervishes. The 21st Lancers, sent to harass the enemy's right, galloped along what seemed to be a thin line of Dervish riflemen. Wheeling in to charge, the Lancers found a packed mass of spearmen thousands strong behind, through which they fought. Reforming beyond, they dismounted and fired their carbines until the Dervishes retreated – to Churchill's disappointment, for he wanted another charge. As it was, although they won three Victoria Crosses, the Lancers suffered 60 casualties out of 310 in a heroic but, as Churchill later admitted, 'futile' episode. In the fighting Churchill had used his pistol instead of a sabre, 'firing in their faces, and killing several'. This probably saved his life. 'How easy to kill a man', he reflected later. The battle decided the war, for about 10,000 Dervishes were killed for a loss of only about 500 of Kitchener's troops.

In what was to be a typical Churchillian attitude, once Khartoum had fallen he wanted mercy for the conquered. He was appalled by the inhuman treatment of the Dervish wounded and the desecration of the Mahdi's tomb, both actions permitted by Kitchener. In his articles and in his book *The River War*, Churchill denounced such actions as 'foul deeds', and praised the Dervishes, calling them 'as brave men as ever walked the earth'. This did not endear him to Kitchener, who did not mention him in despatches. He also called for the peaceful development of the Sudan, and the harnessing of the Nile waters so that 'every drop of water … preserved from evaporation or discharge, shall be equally and amicably divided among the river-peoples'. Such benevolent visions throughout underlay his attitude to imperialism, which he saw as benefiting the ruled as much as the rulers.

Churchill returned to India late in 1898, working on *The River War* that winter and winning the Meerut Inter-regimental Polo Tournament. Then, deciding that the army did not offer enough scope compared to politics, he resigned his commission in March 1899. When he left India, he had finished 18 out of his book's 23 chapters. Published in the autumn and dedicated to Lord Salisbury, it received favourable reviews from the *Manchester Guardian*, the main Liberal newspaper, for his 'chivalrous attitude … towards the enemy' while the Conservative *Times* decried his 'bumptious self-assertion'. But it was as a Conservative that he fought a by-election at Oldham in July, being narrowly defeated. He was unworried by this, for other, even more exciting avenues were opening up.

By September, war between the Boer republics in southern Africa and the British was clearly imminent. Churchill was employed as War Correspondent by the *Morning Post* at £250 per month – a then unprecedented salary. He sailed for the Cape on 14 October. On the same ship was the *Manchester Guardian*'s correspondent J. B. Atkins who described Churchill at the time as 'slim, slightly reddish-haired, pale, lively, frequently plunging along the deck with neck out-thrust … I had not before encountered this sort of ambition, unabashed, frankly egotistical, communicating its excitement'. At Durban, Churchill was invited by a friend from India, Captain Aylmer Haldane, to join an armoured train inland. The Boers, on the offensive, ambushed it. The front coaches were derailed but the engine in the middle was undamaged. Churchill persuaded the wounded driver to shunt the front carriages out of the way, which took an hour under heavy fire, while he organized the line clearance outside. The engine got away but Churchill, who had returned to help Haldane – leaving his Mauser on the train – was captured by the Boers.

Captivity as a POW suited Churchill even less than most men. At first he assumed that, as a journalist, he would be freed, but the Boers realized his role in helping the engine escape and kept him a prisoner, only deciding to release him after some weeks. By then Churchill was gone. Along with Haldane and another officer, he planned an escape via a lavatory. Churchill got out, but the other two could not make it – later they accused him of abandoning them, but he clearly could not afford to hang around. With a bar of chocolate and £75 in his pockets, but no map, compass or word of Afrikaans, he set off through Pretoria, the Boer capital, jumping onto a slow train going east. Thanks to help from some British miners, he made his way to neutral Mozambique and then caught a ship to Durban. He arrived on 23 December 1899 to a hero's welcome 'received as if I had won a great victory'. His escape was a much-needed bit of good news in a year of British catastrophes.

Churchill persuaded the British Commander-in-Chief, Redvers Buller, to let him combine the roles of soldier and journalist again – against army regulations – and reported on most of the events of the next year, which saw the Boers checked if not crushed. He himself fought in several actions, including the capture of Pretoria where he joyfully liberated the POW camp he had been in. By the summer of 1900, however, he was keen to return to Britain and contest a Parliamentary seat in the forthcoming 'Khaki Election'.

3 Into Parliament

When Churchill returned to England to take part in the General Election of September 1900, he was greeted as a hero because of his well-publicized exploits in South Africa. The election was called a 'Khaki Election' not because many soldiers returned home to vote in it – most were still fighting the Boers in Africa – but because the Conservative government could exploit seemingly notable victories such as the relief of Mafeking and Ladysmith. In fact, the war was to drag on for almost two years.

The Conservatives in the textile town of Oldham, Lancashire, where Churchill had already fought and narrowly lost a by-election in 1899, were happy to have him back as a candidate. He stood as a Conservative, rather than Liberal (the other main party), chiefly through loyalty to his father's memory. However, his own views, like Lord Randolph's, were far from typically Tory. 'I am a Liberal in all but name', he had written to his mother from India in 1897. 'Were it not for Irish Home Rule – to which I shall never consent – I would enter Parliament as a Liberal. As it is, Tory Democracy will have to be the standard under which I shall range myself.' (Deep divisions over granting Home Rule to Ireland, then entirely governed from Westminster, had caused some Liberal MPs led by Joseph Chamberlain to leave their party and join the Conservatives as 'Liberal Unionists' ten years earlier. Lord Randolph had, typically perversely, championed the rights of the Ulster Protestants to be excluded from what would become a predominantly Catholic Ireland. The problem of Anglo-Irish relations was to dog and at times dominate British home politics until 1922, due to the many Irish Nationalist MPs sitting in Westminster.) Appropriately Chamberlain himself, then Colonial Secretary, came down to speak on Churchill's behalf.

Boosted by the happy discovery that the wife of a miner who had helped him escape in South Africa was in the audience one night, Churchill won the electors' hearts and enough votes in the double-seated constituency to be narrowly elected, along with a Liberal. He then set off on a frenetic lecture tour of Britain, the United States and Canada, captivating huge audiences with tales of his exploits in South Africa. He earned about £10,000 and met President McKinley and the future president Theodore Roosevelt. Such a large sum of money allowed him – in the days when MPs were not paid – to devote his future energies to politics, as well as helping support his profligate mother, who had just married a handsome but dim and penniless officer, George Cornwallis-West, almost her son's age.

In February 1901, Churchill made his maiden speech in the House of Commons, speaking from his father's old place. This marked the start of a long, chequered but finally glorious parliamentary career. With the exception of the years 1922–24, he was an MP for 63 years and made an estimated 2,000 major speeches, being the last great traditional parliamentary orator, but he was not a typical parliamentarian. His speeches, all carefully composed and then memorized beforehand, tended to be given *to* the House rather than from within it, as though he were addressing a public meeting. Throughout his career his inability to adapt his speech according to the swiftly changing moods of the House – to 'speak on his feet' – could have disastrous effects. In 1904 he lost the thread of a speech he was making in the Commons and rambled inanely, leading some MPs to wonder if he was suffering a mental collapse in the same way his father had done. After that he always took care to have his notes with him. He would rehearse his speeches in front of a few friends or even declaim in his bath or while out walking, to the astonishment of those who overheard him. Generally his wit, vision and stirring if old-fashioned rhetoric elevated his speeches above those of any contemporary. Many still read superbly, especially his disregarded warnings of the 1930s against Hitler.

In his first speech, he dutifully defended British policy in South Africa, but added, 'If I were a Boer, I hope I should be fighting in the field.' Such unorthodox sentiments did not please some Tories, but he ended gracefully thanking the House for its attention 'extended not on my own account but because of a certain splendid memory which many honourable members still preserve' – that of his father. Like Lord Randolph, Churchill soon found cause to disagree with the Conservative government's defence plans. In May he attacked proposals to increase the standing army from two corps to three, with three more in reserve, as 'costly trumpery, dangerous military playthings'. Europe, he claimed in a later speech, 'is now groaning beneath the weight of armies. There is scarcely a single important government whose finances are not embarrassed [by military spending]'. He persuaded 17 other Conservative MPs to vote against the 1901 army reform proposals, effectively killing them. As a recently serving soldier, his views carried weight despite his extreme youth. He always believed, however, in maintaining Britain's supremacy at sea, keeping the Royal Navy up to strength. With its navy unchallengeable by any other, Britain should never need large armies, he reckoned.

Such powerful attacks from a new MP on their own side did not make Churchill popular with his leaders. Any hopes he might have had of office under the Prime Minister Arthur Balfour were dashed. He was linked instead with five young Tory rebels nicknamed the 'Hughligans' because they were led by the eccentric Lord Hugh Cecil, son of Lord Salisbury. Rather than adding to Britain's armies, which would not anyway be large enough to begin to match the great Continental forces of Germany, France and Russia, Churchill proposed strengthening the nation by peaceful state-backed schemes to relieve poverty and improve public health and education – proposals more Liberal than 'Tory Democrat'.

Already, his hankering for a non-partisan or middle party was emerging in ideas for a coalition of 'Tory-Liberals'. This could consist of Liberal Unionists like Joseph Chamberlain and the Duke of

Devonshire – both actually in the Conservative government at the time – along with leading Liberals such as Lord Rosebery, a former Prime Minister, or Sir Edward Grey, who supported the government over the war in South Africa. Rosebery listened sympathetically to the ideas Churchill propounded over the dinner tables of political London, but others were not so taken, either by the man or the politician, regarding his ideas as impractical to the point of being fantastical.

Churchill certainly loved talking – was indeed intoxicated by words – but he was less interested in conversing with other guests than in talking at them. The society hostess Etie Grenfell complained that 'Winston leads general conversation on the hearth rug, addressing himself in the looking glass – a sympathetic and admiring audience'. Despite his transparent egotism and physically unimposing presence – he was only 5ft 7 and still skinny, though proud of his 'aristocratically' small white hands and feet – some women were intrigued by his obvious drive, vision and sheer gusto for life. At this time he was fox-hunting, gambling (on holiday at Deauville in France, where he sometimes stayed at the tables till 5 a.m.), eating and drinking heavily (he was especially fond of cognac) and spending a lot of money on clothes, including silk underwear for his sensitive skin. But Churchill was for long ultra-cautious with unmarried women, paying attention only to those safely married, again to his hostesses' annoyance. This was chiefly due to shyness, but his father's terrible example cannot have encouraged sexual adventures.

Churchill was involved in a major literary project at this time: a biography of Lord Randolph. For this act of filial piety he was given access to the Blenheim Palace archives and to Lord Rosebery's own papers; he already possessed his father's diaries and letters as his heir. Most of the politicians who had supported or opposed his father were still alive and proved surprisingly willing to help him, including Conservatives such as Joseph Chamberlain with whom Churchill had by then quarrelled. He completed the first draft in 1904 which was read by Rosebery among others. Macmillan, the publishers, offered him

£8,000 (then a vast advance) and the book appeared in January 1906, at the height of the general election campaign.

Churchill had set out to vindicate his father's memory, and he toned down many of his father's more vehement speeches. He said little about Lord Randolph's private life and nothing about his fatal syphilis, a subject contemporaries preferred to ignore. Instead, he stressed the radicalism of Lord Randolph's 'Tory Democracy' which increasingly attracted working-class voters and was to help make the Conservatives the dominant party of the twentieth century. The book was widely praised, even by those unconvinced by Churchill's central claim that Lord Randolph had been unjustly treated by Salisbury and the rest of the Conservative hierarchy. The *Spectator* said 'it avoided the pitfalls of the partisan' and the historian A.F. Pollard wrote perceptively: 'Its solid merits raise hopes that Mr Churchill is gifted with greater staying power than his brilliant but neurotic father possessed.'

In May 1903, Joseph Chamberlain, not Churchill, broke the mould of British politics – for the second time in his unusually destructive career. Speaking in Birmingham, Chamberlain called for a policy of 'Imperial Preference', meaning trade protection for British industries within the huge empire, which would supply raw materials to Britain in exchange for manufactured goods, while high tariffs would discriminate against imports from other countries. British industry, once unchallenged, had been losing out to newer rivals such as Germany and the US since the 1880s, causing increasing concern. But free trade had long been accepted as one of the pillars of British greatness and wealth. (Agriculture, too, was going through a long, deep depression, but this was considered less worrying in an industrial nation.)

Chamberlain's speech proved deeply divisive, shaking the Conservative party to its core. In Churchill's words, 'a hurricane of disputation raged through the land'. He had already made his own views clear in October 1902 in a speech in Oldham: 'What protection means is that all the people of this country subscribe together through the taxes to make a payment towards keeping certain trades going ... Every trade in the land would agitate for protective assistance ... Protection would not help the cotton trade in any way ... I cannot understand a Lancashire man favouring a general system of Protection.' He spoke out with characteristic decisiveness on the subject, at a time when Balfour was still trying to paper over divisions. Some other Conservatives agreed with Churchill, however, including Lord Hugh Cecil and the Duke of Devonshire, who resigned from the Cabinet in protest against Balfour's failure to stand firm against the Tariff Reformers (Chamberlain's supporters). Churchill and Lord Hugh formed a Unionist (Conservative) Free Food League to fight Chamberlain, but their speeches met increasing hostility from Conservative audiences. By late 1903 Balfour's government seemed likely to fall but it hung on, to Churchill's open disappointment.

'The position which many moderate reasonable people occupy is one of great difficulty', he wrote at this time in the *Monthly Review*. Increasingly he felt drawn to the Liberals and in December 1903 sent a letter of support to a Liberal candidate at Ludlow which lost him the Conservative Whip (i.e. he ceased to be considered officially part of the Conservative party). He offered to resign his seat at Oldham and fight for re-election as a Free Trade Reformer, but the local Conservatives turned his proposal down. In March 1904 the Conservatives walked out *en masse* during a speech he made in the Commons on free trade. Finally in May, encouraged by Lloyd George, the fiery young Welsh Liberal, he crossed the floor to become a Liberal. Significantly, he again chose a seat once taken by his father, just below the gangway. He was also invited to contest Manchester North-west as a Free Trade candidate at the next election, although retaining his Oldham seat for the present.

Over the next two-and-a-half years Churchill made many fiery speeches defending free trade, but he adopted Liberal views on numerous subjects, from accepting trade unions' legal rights to raise subscriptions (restricted since the Taff Vale case of 1901), to condemning the inhumane treatment of Chinese workers brought to

South Africa to work in the mines but deprived of their families. He also began to commend himself to his new constituency by championing the rights of Jewish immigrants trying to escape pogroms in Russia. Lord Rothschild, his father's old friend, had spoken out against proposed bans on further immigration and Churchill wrote to Nathan Laski, prominent in the Manchester Jewish community, stating that he would fight any measure 'which … smirches those ancient traditions of freedom and hospitality for which Britain has so long been renowned'.

In December 1905, Balfour finally resigned and Campbell-Bannerman formed an interim Liberal government. Churchill was offered the Financial Secretaryship to the Treasury but instead asked for the lesser post of Under-Secretary for the Colonies, where he would be the only minister in the Commons, his superior Lord Elgin being in the Lords. In the January 1906 General Election Churchill contested his Manchester seat as a junior minister – and one much in the public eye. The *Manchester Guardian* reported that his audiences greeted him with 'an enthusiasm which finds no parallel in previous political contests in Manchester'. Accused of being a turncoat, Churchill admitted that he had 'said a lot of stupid things when I worked with the Conservative party, and I left it because I did not want to go on saying stupid things'. This won applause. Most voters in Manchester, a great trading city, enthusiastically accepted his views on Free Trade and he was elected, gaining 5,639 votes to 4,398 for his Conservative opponent. Now at last he could begin to make his way in politics.

4 Churchill the Radical

Churchill was swept back into Parliament in the landslide Liberal victory of January 1906. The new government, first under Campbell Bannerman and then, after 1908, under Asquith, proved to be one of the great reforming governments of the twentieth century, effectively laying the basis of the welfare state. Far from being among the conservatives, Churchill was one of its keenest radicals as President of the Board of Trade and then as Home Secretary. Many at the time questioned the reforming sincerity of this former Tory with such an extremely aristocratic background. Conservatives labelled him 'the rat of Blenheim' and he was blackballed (denied membership) of the Hurlingham Club, where he wanted to play polo, an unusual snub. On the other hand, left-wingers such as Beatrice Webb still thought him 'shallow-minded and reactionary'.

But Churchill's concern for people trapped in poverty was, like most of the views he held at any one time, genuine and deeply felt. He undoubtedly remained always a patrician at heart, intervening high-mindedly from above to help those far below him on the social ladder. He never had any direct experience of working-class poverty, but neither had comfortably middle-class Socialists like the Webbs. He had earlier been shocked by reading Seebohm Rowntree's classic study *Poverty* (1901), which revealed that 40 per cent of the working class was living in poverty. Such findings made 'his hair stand on end'. Once roused, he attacked the problem with his usual energy and passion, blithely making enemies left and right. He obviously wanted to defend the appeal of the Liberal party (still the chief alternative to the Conservatives) to working-class voters against the growing Labour Party. 'Socialism seeks to pull down wealth,' he told an election meeting in 1908, 'Liberalism seeks to raise up poverty'.

He also wanted to build up Britain's national strength, which he realized was threatened by widespread poverty. He saw 'little glory in an Empire which can rule the waves' yet was 'unable to flush its sewers'. 'We want to draw a line below which we will not allow persons to live and labour', he said in 1906. Such rousing rhetoric, along with his ancestry, made him a noted figure and in January 1906, he was made Under-Secretary (junior minister) for the Colonies.

At once he turned his energies towards a South African settlement. With the magnanimity he had already demonstrated towards the defeated Boers, he urged immediate self-government for the Transvaal and Orange Free State – appalling most Conservatives but convincing the Cabinet. In 1907, South Africa became self-governing. Edward VII sent Churchill a telegram congratulating him for putting the interests of his country before his party. Churchill then spent four months travelling round East Africa, exhausting his hosts with endless journeys, inspections and meetings and, like a true Imperialist, advancing the Kenyan frontier 50 miles (80 km). On his return he called for more railways and a dam on the upper Nile to generate electricity. By now he was as renowned for his tireless industry as for his brilliant if often bombastic speech-making. In April 1908, he entered the Cabinet at the age of 33, becoming President of the Board of Trade – a suitable post for a Free Trader.

As there was then no Ministry of Labour, this also gave him a role in social and industrial affairs, but first he had to recontest his seat, the current custom for new Cabinet ministers. Surprisingly, he lost – to a Conservative – but Dundee's Liberals invited him to represent them and he won the election there with ease. Churchill took over his post from Lloyd George who, as the new Chancellor of the Exchequer, so often collaborated with Churchill that they were called the 'two Romeos'. Lloyd George was impressed by Germany's Labour Exchanges and Churchill, capably assisted by William Beveridge, a young Oxford don, and William Masterman, Under-Secretary for Local Government, planned a similar British system for the whole country. This proved uncontentious and in May 1909 Churchill's eloquently presented bill was almost unopposed in the Commons. In the same year he set up Trade Boards to regulate the wages and hours of 'sweated labour' – non-unionized workers in tailoring, lace-making, paperbox-making and chain-making. These Boards, later known as Wage Councils, were soon expanded to cover many more industries.

Such reforms were badly needed, for 1908 saw another trade depression that hit many workers. Churchill wanted to start a compulsory National Insurance Scheme, again on German lines, for the unemployed. This potentially costly idea fell foul of storms over the Budget. To pay for the proposed Old Age Pensions, Lloyd George had introduced a radical Budget in March 1909 including increases in income tax and death duties and a revolutionary tax on unearned increases in land values. The last proved too much for the House of Lords, still filled with large landowners, who rejected the Finance Bill – the first time they had done such a thing in over 200 years – so sparking a constitutional crisis. No compromise could be reached and Asquith dissolved Parliament. Churchill, who had rousingly defended the Budget in the Commons, became chairman of the Budget League. He toured the country making speeches under the slogan 'The Peers against the People', attacking – in typically extreme language – the Lords as 'a played-out, obsolete anachronistic assembly' and calling for their drastic reform, if not abolition. These were strange sentiments for a duke's grandson but consistent with his current sincere radicalism. They made him even more unpopular with the Tories while most Liberals still distrusted him. Strangely, Churchill never sought to build up a power base among MPs, relying instead on his unrivalled drive and oratory, which could generally sway MPs and voters alike at any given moment. But fellow ministers could find this love of his own voice and inability to listen to others irritating. 'His great weakness', remarked Masterman perceptively, 'is his love of the limelight'.

The Liberals were returned with a reduced majority in January 1910, becoming dependent on Irish Nationalist MPs to govern. This meant that the ever-simmering issue of Irish Home Rule was back on the agenda. Churchill now supported the concept of Irish Home Rule, as did most Liberals, if with some reservations about its implementation. The Lords finally accepted the Finance Bill but Asquith introduced a Parliament Bill to cripple their future powers and the crisis dragged on, with another inconclusive General Election in October. In April, Churchill had become Home Secretary – officially the senior post after Prime Minister, a notable achievement for a man still only 35. He turned to prison reform and, mindful of how soul-destroying his own brief prison experience in South Africa had been, allowed prisoners books and entertainments such as concerts. He also reduced the maximum time normally spent in solitary confinement to one month and tried to reduce exceptionally long prison sentences for non-violent offenders. Two serious coal mining accidents in 1910 – at Whitehaven, Cumberland, where 132 men died, and Bolton, Lancashire, where 320 died – turned his attentions to regulating working conditions underground. Strict rules concerning ventilation, the use of electricity and explosives and haulage systems were introduced in the Mines Act of 1911, and boys under 14 were no longer to be employed underground. He also introduced a Shops Bill to help shop workers, restricting their working hours to 60 per week, ensuring girls had a seat behind their counters and giving them all a half-day off, although only the last measure got passed.

On one major issue, however, he failed to show reforming zeal: the suffragettes and their long-drawn campaign, which was marked by increasingly dramatic acts of civil disobedience, to win women the vote. Although his wife Clementine sympathized with them, Churchill was ambivalent. His essentially romantic view of women did not easily encompass them as equal partners in political life. More pertinently, like many in the Liberal Cabinet, he worried that if women were accepted on the current household franchise – which gave most, but not all, men the vote – only wealthier women would be enfranchized, and this could help the Conservatives electorally. In 1910 he changed his mind about supporting a bill for women's suffrage on the existing franchise, saying: 'It is an undemocratic bill ... it gives an entirely unfair representation to property as against persons.' This refusal lost him some good friends such as Lord Lytton, whose sister was a leading suffragette. In November 1910, when 300 women demonstrating at Westminister were maltreated by the police in what was called 'Black Friday', Churchill as Home Secretary was blamed. Like all members of the Cabinet he was frequently abused by suffragettes and their male sympathizers, and sometimes physically threatened. Physical violence did not worry him at all, but his reputation as a social reformer was to be damaged more seriously and more lastingly by other events in which he was depicted as a bloodthirsty reactionary.

In November 1910 striking coal miners in Tonypandy, South Wales, rioted. Troops were sent out but Churchill halted them *en route*, ordering that they should 'not come into direct contact with rioters unless and until action has been taken by the police'. In fact, the police dealt with the rioters using nothing more than their rolled-up mackintoshes and not a shot was fired. Nonetheless, a 'Tonypandy myth' soon grew up that Churchill had ordered troops to fire on the strikers. Keir Hardie, the Labour leader, attacked him in the Commons for this. From then on Churchill was seen as an 'enemy of the working class', an inaccurate title which would have upset a more sensitive man. But his reputation as a man who relished dramatic, even violent action was better founded. In January 1911 he was photographed, in his top hat, peering round the corner as the police besieged three gunmen, desperate jewel thieves, in a house in Sidney Street in the East End of London. When rebuked for his superfluous presence there, quite inappropriate for a Home Secretary, he confessed disarmingly: 'It was such fun.'

In August 1911 a far more serious wave of strikes developed in docks across the country, which threatened to bring the country to a standstill when the railway workers joined in. This national crisis appealed to Churchill as a man of action and he began vigorously dispatching troops around the country, even sending them to Manchester where they had not been asked for. When in Liverpool the police could not control the rioters and requested the army be sent in, Churchill sent in the navy too, ordering the cruiser HMS *Antrim* to the docks. This show of force backfired, for Lloyd George had mediated an end to the strike already. An angry crowd at Llanelli, Wales, then blocked a train driven by blackleg (strike-breaking) labour and in the resulting confusion two men were shot by soldiers.

Several Liberals, including the Lord Chancellor, Lord Loreburn, thought Churchill's actions 'irresponsible' and the *Manchester Guardian*, until then among his keenest supporters, criticized him too. In the circumstances Asquith thought it wiser to move Churchill to the Admiralty, where his bellicosity might be better directed against Britain's external rather than internal enemies. He became First Lord of the Admiralty (head of the navy) in October 1911, a timely move, for internationally the situation was deteriorating gravely.

The Admiralty and the Dardanelles

5

Churchill's move to First Lord of the Admiralty was not a promotion, for the Home Secretary was the higher post, but it offered him a far more congenial role than dealing with strikers or suffragettes. Soon he was 'burrowing about in an illimitable rabbit-warren', as he put it, with his usual vigour. Reforming and modernizing the navy was by now considered as urgent by the government as anything at home, for the Royal Navy, still the 'senior service', was facing its greatest challenge for a century.

Since Nelson had crushed the French navy at the Battle of Trafalgar in 1805, Britain had 'ruled the waves' with a confident ease bordering on complacency, patrolling the global seas with a navy equal in size at least to the next two biggest navies combined. This naval pre-eminence was considered essential to protect an empire by then spread right around the world. But in 1898 Germany, previously only a land power with few overseas colonies, began building a vast new navy, so starting an arms race. Britain could easily win any such race, for she was still the greatest ship-building nation. In 1906 the Dreadnought, first of an entirely new, far more powerful type of battleship, was launched, at once making all other battleships obsolete. A row developed over how many more should be built. The Admiralty wanted eight. Asquith at first suggested only four but finally gave way to popular demand expressed in the chant: 'We want eight and we won't wait.'

Churchill was not at that time keen on increasing naval expenditure, nor did he consider Germany a threat to Britain. In 1908 he said of Anglo-German relations: 'Although there may be snapping and snarling in the newspapers ... these two great peoples have nothing to fight about.' That year Churchill was impressed by observing (as a guest) the German army on its annual manoeuvres. 'A terrible engine.

It marches sometimes 35 miles a day. It is in numbers as the sands of the sea', he wrote awed, but Germany, with its excellent social security system, still seemed to him a model, not a rival. With Lloyd George, he opposed the Admiralty's plans for new battleships in 1909. But in August 1911, while still Home Secretary, he showed remarkable prescience by predicting how a war between the great powers would start: a German offensive would sweep through Belgium towards Paris, and the British would have to rush to help the French army's left flank by dispatching 100,000 troops.

This revolution in his views was due to a new twist in the arms race initiated by the German admiral Tirpitz's attempts to match British strength in Dreadnoughts, and even more by the Agadir Crisis. In July 1911 the Germans sent a cruiser, the *Panther*, to Agadir in Morocco to intimidate France that was, by international agreement, establishing a protectorate over the country. The Germans themselves wanted north African colonies. Britain, in the person of Lloyd George, issued a stern warning to Germany, which backed down. But the crisis, and the latent German aggressiveness revealed by it, helped convert the informal 'Triple Entente' of France, Britain and Russia into something far more like a genuine military alliance. A feeling that war was likely was growing in political circles, but the prospect did not depress Churchill, whose martial spirit thrilled to being 'piped aboard' great battleships and being among fighting men again. However, he found much at the Admiralty that displeased him.

Even before taking up his post Churchill had damned the Admiralty as 'cocksure, insouciant and apathetic'. Admiral Sir John Fisher, the dynamic if choleric First Sea Lord (highest admiral) who had introduced the Dreadnought battleships and the first submarines, had resigned in frustration in 1910. Churchill, an admirer and friend of Fisher, with whom he corresponded, was unimpressed by his more cautious successor Arthur Wilson, and managed to have the radical Prince Louis Battenberg made Second Sea Lord (second in command). These relatively young men set out to introduce new ideas and new technologies in the teeth of naval conservatism. When an admiral objected that some proposed reforms of discipline went against the Royal Navy's hallowed traditions, Churchill reputedly dismissed these as 'rum, sodomy and the lash'. Such outspokenness was unpopular, as were his actions in interfering in gunnery practice on manoeuvres in 1912, his habit of personally berating officers for lapses in front of their men, listening to junior officers' complaints and introducing a channel of promotion for ordinary seamen into the ranks of officers. He also got rid of ancient punishments for sailors, such as being 'stood in the corner', and raised their modest pay. All this appealed to ordinary sailors but struck senior officers as dangerously radical. However, many of his other reforms were to prove vital in the coming World War.

Most significantly, Churchill hastened the equipment of newly-built battleships of the Queen Elizabeth class with the 15-inch gun, which was far more powerful than the original Dreadnoughts' 12-inch. He also authorized the fleet to switch from burning coal to oil. This enabled ships to sail faster and for longer than earlier, oil being a more concentrated fuel than coal, although at the cost of making the navy dependent on imported fuel. To safeguard oil supplies, the government bought control of the Anglo-Persian Oil Company (today BP), which proved a brilliant investment. Churchill also encouraged, as far as budgetary restraints permitted, the development of the Fleet Air Arm, with innovative seaplanes and even designs for an aircraft carrier, then very radical. He himself flew several times, piloting aircrafts with a verve that alarmed his young wife Clementine, for air travel was then in its dangerous infancy. He also supported the development of submarines, although failing like most at the time to appreciate fully the threat they posed to battleships.

One of his most far-sighted reforms was the establishment in January 1912 of a Naval War Staff, comparable to the army's, with a college at Portsmouth, arranged in three divisions: Operations, Intelligence and Mobilization. This again annoyed naval traditionalists, who saw no need for it. Unfortunately, war came before this reform had time to have much effect. Churchill appointed Admiral Sir John Jellicoe as Second-in-Command of the North Sea-based Home Fleet, so ensuring that he would soon become its Commander. Churchill also employed the relatively young (40 years old) Rear-Admiral David Beatty as his Personal Navy Secretary – his own, as it turned out, highly inspired choice. Both officers were to play crucial roles in the coming war. Combined, these reforms kept the Royal Navy superior to any in the world. Without them, Britain might have lost the coming war.

What really angered Conservatives in the Commons was Churchill's rearranging of the naval squadrons. Traditionally the Mediterranean fleet was the largest, safeguarding the essential route to India. Churchill, aware of the growing threat from Germany, decided to cut it to strengthen the Home Fleet in the North Sea, with France taking on the chief role in the Mediterranean. This latter point worried many Liberals who did not want Britain tied to a formal alliance with France and Churchill was forced to compromise, keeping the Mediterranean fleet equal to any other fleet *after* France's, while calling the talks with the French 'informal'.

All this hard work – Eddie Marsh, his secretary, joked that Churchill had made a new commandment, 'The Seventh Day is the Sabbath of the First Lord, on it thou shalt do all manner of work' – did not stop Churchill enjoying himself. A perk of the post was the 3,500-ton Admiralty yacht, the *Enchantress*, on which at times Churchill almost lived, sailing round the coast. In 1912 he invited Asquith and his family on a long Mediterranean cruise on it. He also enjoyed wearing the many different uniforms that his roles permitted, including that of an Elder (honorary) Brother of Trinity House, the lighthouse organization. This last role led him to remark to a French general in his distinctive French, 'Je suis un frère aîné de la Trinité' ('I am an elder brother of the Trinity'). The general reputedly congratulated him on having divine relations.

Despite his preoccupation with the navy, Churchill was also involved in the most pressing issue of the day: Irish Home Rule, which Liberal governments had been trying to effect for 30 years. The problem now was not obstruction by the Tory-ruled House of Lords, which could no longer veto bills, only delay them, but the Ulster Unionists, northern Protestants who refused to be part of a mainly Catholic Ireland. In February 1912, Churchill and Clementine visited Belfast to speak to the Ulster Liberal Association – a brave, even foolhardy move, as the Unionists mobbed and almost overturned his car, although many Catholics turned out to listen to him. Churchill proposed 'Home Rule All Round', a federal rearranging of the whole United Kingdom. This proved unacceptable and Churchill moved towards the idea of excluding Ulster somehow from Ireland. But by early 1914 the Ulster Unionists were clearly drilling for war, as were the Irish Nationalists. Asquith's government decided to send troops to suppress them, but many British troops, especially the officers, were sympathetic to the Ulstermen. They refused to march in what became known as the Curragh mutiny. An all-party conference summoned by the King in July failed to resolve the issues, until a far greater war overshadowed them.

In January 1913, Churchill had formally proposed to Germany that both countries should freeze their arms race, but the Germans had not replied. In 1914 he urged a great expansion of the battle-fleet, which his Cabinet colleagues almost rejected as too costly. Bitter wrangles led to him getting his way but, as a compromise, he agreed to a trial mobilization of the Home Fleet that summer rather than more expensive full manoeuvres. When on 24 July, at the end of this trial, he heard of the Austrian demands on Serbia, which the Serbs could not accept without jeopardizing their independence, he decided to keep the fleet at battle stations, rather than letting the ships disperse. This proved one of his wisest moves. Britain, like the rest of Europe, was still at peace but attempts at a diplomatic solution failed and on 30 July Austro-Hungary declared war on Serbia. Russia then came to Serbia's aid, Germany to Austro-Hungary's and France to Russia's. Britain had no formal alliance with any continental power but had promised to defend Belgian neutrality. When the Germans marched into Belgium on 4 August, heading for France, the Cabinet decided almost unanimously on war. Churchill, on his own initiative, had already mobilized the navy, so seizing the initiative.

Although there were still major deficiencies in naval equipment – primarily lack of good ammunition and anti-submarine defences – Churchill's short time at the Admiralty had transformed the navy, as even enemies such as the German naval attaché admitted. His actions over the next year were to be less admired, but at first all went well. Although some German cruisers remained at large to threaten British commerce, a German flotilla was defeated on 27 August in the North Sea, leading to the Kaiser (German Emperor) ordering the whole German fleet to remain in port. From then on, a steady blockade of Germany was maintained, which finally caused its economic collapse in 1918.

Churchill, however, was concerned with matters closer to home. The German offensive in August almost reached Paris before being repulsed. Both sides began pushing towards the coast in September, the British being desperate to keep the Germans away from the Channel. The Belgians still defending Antwerp, their chief port, announced on 2 October that they would have to surrender without help. Churchill, who had been overseeing air defences on the French coast (there was no separate RAF yet) and organizing patrols by Rolls Royces converted into armoured cars, drove across Belgium and took over the defence of Antwerp on the 3 October, with the Belgians' agreement. Setting up his headquarters in the city's best hotel, he galvanized its defence. But the Cabinet in London treated his request to be made a general commanding there as a joke – 'Winston is an ex-lieutenant!' said Asquith – and after he left Antwerp fell to the Germans on 10 October. The affair led to attacks on Churchill for foolhardiness.

As the war in France became one of bloody stalemate in the trenches, growing anti-German feeling at home forced the resignation of Prince Louis of Battenberg as First Sea Lord because of his German name. He was replaced by Fisher, 73 years old but still amazingly energetic, who at first complemented Churchill's dynamism perfectly. Victory in the Battle of the Falkland Islands in November, when von Spee's marauding battle-cruiser squadron was annihilated by the British, restored the navy's and Churchill's reputation – for a while.

Turkey, a German ally, was threatening Egypt (vital because of the Suez Canal) and also blockading the Russian Black Sea ports, essential for supplying Russian armies. Churchill suggested that an attack on the Dardanelles, the narrow strait connecting the Aegean and Marmora seas, would open the way for a direct bombardment of the Turkish capital Constantinople (Istanbul) and knock Turkey out of the war. The idea was strategically brilliant. The problem lay in its implementation, for the Turks had fortified the straits heavily. Fisher, doubtful from the first, thought the navy could not do the job without soldiers in support, but Churchill persuaded the Cabinet that battleships alone could force a passage through the straits. Unfortunately, the ships sent to the Dardanelles in February 1915 started the bombardment haphazardly, breaking off in bad weather. The main threat to the ships came from Turkish mines, not guns, three British and two French battleships being sunk early in March – a not unexpected loss, but a fruitless one, as the Turkish guns were still firing. The Cabinet agreed to land troops to help demolish the forts, but delays in transporting them from Egypt and France, due to delays by General Kitchener, the War Minister, gave the Turks time to reinforce their defences. When British, Australian, French and New Zealander troops began landing on the peninsula around Gallipoli on 25 April, they were trapped near the beaches by Turkish fire and never captured the central ridge. A second larger landing in August proved no more successful. The campaign to break the Western Front deadlock was deadlocked itself. By the time Allied troops were finally withdrawn in December 1915, they had suffered 250,000 casualties and gained nothing.

Meanwhile in London, Fisher had resigned, leaving Churchill to take all the blame. Simultaneously Asquith's government faced a crisis of confidence, due both to the developing disaster at Gallipoli and to a scandal over ammunition shortages for the army in France – the fault mainly of Kitchener. This forced it to seek a coalition with the Conservatives led by Bonar Law. One of the Conservative conditions for entering a coalition was that Churchill, unforgiven for his 'treachery', must go. Weakened by the Dardanelles fiasco for which he was held mainly responsible, Churchill was demoted on 22 May to Chancellor of Duchy of Lancaster, an honorific post, Balfour replacing him at the Admiralty. He accepted his demotion with dignity, thanking all serving him at the Admiralty in person, but it was an unexpected blow. He had not realized how little support he had in the Liberal Party, nor how unpopular he still was with many Tories. He spent a depressed six months on the sidelines, watching 'the unhappy casting-away of plans which I had launched and in which I had heartily believed'. In November 1915 he finally left the Government and went to France to fight in the trenches. The first phase of his political career had ended, in something like total failure.

A Tory Once More

6

Churchill plunged into trench warfare with his customary gusto, positively relishing the sound of gunfire. After a month's 'apprenticeship' as major in the Scots Guard (he had actually become a major in the Territorial Army before the war), in December 1915 he became Lieutenant-Colonel of the 6th Battalion of the Scottish Royal Fusiliers. Immediate higher commands such as Major-General, which he had half-expected, were considered to smack of undue favouritism. The battalion – about 600 men – was stationed just inside Belgium. It had suffered the usual high casualties and was resting when Churchill arrived.

Churchill soon made himself popular with his officers by his fascinating conversation in the mess – one of them noted an understandable bitterness about Asquith – and by lending them his tin bath, one of his few special luxuries. His men appreciated the way he made visiting VIPs stumble through the mud of the trenches, getting their shiny boots filthy, and his vigorous delousing campaign. Their section of the Front was relatively quiet at the time – although Churchill called on a friendly artillery officer to lay on the odd bombardment to which the Germans would retaliate – and he had time to write a paper expounding the advantages of 'landships', caterpillar-tracked vehicles which he had first authorized building at the Admiralty. In March 1916, while on leave, he attended a debate in the Commons (he was still an MP) and severely criticized Balfour, his successor at the Admiralty. He astonished everybody by calling for the return to the Admiralty of Fisher, whose resignation had thrown the blame for the Dardanelles onto him.

Churchill increasingly felt that he himself had to return to politics. When the battalion was amalgamated with another in May 1916 he gave up his commission and returned to Westminster. He remained, however, without office. Although earning £1,000 from articles in the *Sunday Pictorial*, he was short of money at the time, and the Churchills had to move out of their house in Eccleston Square when the lease expired in 1918. In his articles he attacked the Somme offensive in France, which began in July 1916 and swiftly became a disaster dwarfing Gallipoli. He gave trenchant evidence in his own defence to the Dardanelles Commission in October 1916, which partly exonerated him when published in January 1917. But his speeches were still interrupted by cries of 'What about the Dardanelles?' When Lloyd George replaced Asquith as Prime Minister in December 1916, the hatred of many Tories kept him from giving Churchill office as expected. 'The insensate fury they displayed [to Churchill] …', wrote Lloyd George, 'surpassed all my apprehensions, and … swelled to the dimensions of a grave ministerial crisis, which threatened the life of the government'. Even so, by May 1917 he was discussing Cabinet affairs with Churchill.

The year 1917 was unpromising for the Allies, despite the entry of the United States into the war in April. The Russian Revolution threatened to weaken the Eastern Front, while on the Western Front the Germans retreated to the almost impregnable prepared defences of the Hindenburg Line. There were mutinies in the French army and war weariness in Britain. Although the German economy was being slowly strangled by the British blockade, its industries still seemed able to produce more munitions than the Allies. Lloyd George, therefore, decided to risk Tory wrath and make Churchill Minister of Munitions of War in July 1917 – but without a seat in the Cabinet.

Churchill showed his usual energetic application as minister, galvanizing his huge bureaucracy of 12,000 people and the large labour force it commanded, increasing the efficiency of the 'gigantic agencies for the slaughter of men by machinery'. He tried to improve labour relations by giving skilled workers a 12.5 per cent pay rise. W. C. Anderson, an otherwise critical Labour MP, admitted that Churchill had 'brought courage and a certain quality of imagination to … labour relations'. To provide extra munitions needed to cope with the German spring offensive that year, many workers worked through the Easter Bank Holiday. Typically, Churchill studied the army's needs in France at first hand. This allowed him to make numerous trips to the Front – often by aeroplane, once almost crashing into the Channel – where he hobnobbed with generals who appreciated his vigour. A letter from Hague, the British Commander-in-Chief, thanked him for his 'energy and foresight … as Minister of Munitions'. This was written just after the decisive Battle of Amiens in August 1918, when tanks were first used *en masse* as he had long urged, smashing through the German lines. Soon after, German armies began to crumble all along the Front, while in Germany mutinies and riots led the new Prime Minister, Prince Max of Baden, to sue for peace.

On Armistice Day, 11 November 1918, after Germany's final collapse, Churchill drove with Clementine through cheering crowds to Downing Street to have dinner with the Prime Minister. Lloyd George wanted to hang the Kaiser, among other reparation measures, but Churchill, never a vindictive man, disagreed. Instead, he called for a programme of domestic 'peaceful reconstruction', which included radical measures such as nationalizing the railways and minimum wages. But the double post he accepted in January 1919 in the post-war Cabinet was Secretary of State for War and Air Minister. His first concern was to demobilize the army. Near mutiny had greeted earlier proposals to let men with the most important skills out first, irrespective of their length of service. Churchill scrapped this in favour of schemes related to military service actually performed, defusing an ugly crisis.

In 1919, Churchill grew obsessed with the 'Red peril'. After the second Russian Revolution in October 1917, British troops had landed at Murmansk and other Russian ports to safeguard arms supplies sent earlier for the Tsarist government. In 1919 Russia slid into civil war between the Communists in Moscow and various anti-Bolshevik White generals round the borders. Churchill wanted to intervene militarily to rid the world of the 'plague bacillus of Bolshevism'. British troops, however, had had enough war and none in the Cabinet shared Churchill's passionate anti-Bolshevism. Arms, but not troops, were sent to help the White generals. Lloyd George joked that 'Churchill's ducal blood revolted against the wholescale elimination of Grand Dukes in Russia' but found his mania embarrassing and told him to desist. This disagreement revealed Churchill out of sympathy with the Liberals and starting to move towards the Conservatives. Labour papers and politicians now revived old charges of him being hostile to the working class while the Tory *Morning Post* began mentioning him favourably. As Lloyd George's coalition contained more Conservatives than Liberals, this did Churchill no harm.

Churchill pushed successfully for the retention of the RAF as a separate body, rather than one amalgamated with the army. When Churchill moved to the Colonial Office in February 1921, he remained Minister for Air, scaling down proposals for a huge new airforce, although a punitive bombing expedition in Somalia in 1920 suggested air power could be cheaper and more effective than using ground forces. In March 1921 he set off with Clementine for Cairo, where he presided over a grand conference to try to settle the Middle East. Much of this area, formerly in the Ottoman Turkish Empire, had been given to Britain as a mandate by the League of Nations (precursor of the UN). Britain wanted control of its oil resources but not the expense of ruling it. Churchill, advised by T. E. Lawrence (of Arabia) with whom he struck up a friendship, agreed to establishing Transjordan (today Jordan) and Iraq as semi-independent kingdoms. Both moves reduced the need for British garrisons. In Palestine, however, he had less success. Although he supported the Balfour Declaration of 1915 promising a Jewish national home in Palestine, he also tried to convince Muslim and Christian Arabs that Britain would safeguard their rights, but they remained sceptical.

A more pressing problem was Ireland. Since the 1916 Easter rising, it had been in open revolt led by Sinn Fein against Britain. As Secretary for War, Churchill had sent in the Black and Tans – soldiers acting as auxiliary policemen, who gained an evil reputation for bloody reprisals – but now he favoured a settlement. In May 1921 negotiations were opened, in July a truce was declared and in October five Sinn Fein representatives came to a London conference. Churchill turned his charm on Michael Collins, leader of the Irish Republican Army. Collins had had a price of £500 put on his head by the British. Churchill pointed out that when he had been wanted by the Boers after his escape in South Africa, he had only been priced at £25. The agreement reached – independence except for Ulster's six counties, but Ireland staying within the British Commonwealth – was rejected by half the Sinn Feiners, resulting in Irish civil war. It was also attacked by the Conservative leader Bonar Law, who had resigned from the Coalition Cabinet, weakening Lloyd George's position. Around this time Churchill revived the idea of a centre party, termed the Fusion Party, to 'combine the patriotism and stability of the Conservative Party with the broad humanities and tolerance of Liberalism', but found little support.

It was another war that wrecked the coalition. Churchill was sympathetic to the national revolution carried out in Turkey under Mustafa Kemal (Ataturk), but Lloyd George favoured the Greeks, waging a war of conquest in Asia Minor. The Turks repulsed the Greek invasion and by September 1922 were threatening the Dardanelles under Franco-British protection. Churchill suddenly changed sides, perhaps finding the Dardanelles a sensitive point, and argued for military action to stop the Turks. He sent the other Commonwealth governments a communiqué announcing his action, taking their support for granted. This annoyed the Canadians especially, and public opinion in Britain showed that further war would be unpopular. The crisis was solved diplomatically, but it showed Churchill once more in a bellicose light and Lloyd George losing his grip.

On 19 October 1922, rebellious Conservative MPs, meeting in the Carlton Club, chose Bonar Law as their leader. Lloyd George's coalition, two-thirds Conservatives, collapsed, Lloyd George resigned and a general election was called. At this critical moment Churchill went down with acute appendicitis and had to have an operation. He sent Clementine up to Dundee to campaign on his behalf but she met abuse and rejection. Churchill himself, turning up frail at the campaign's end, was seen as a warmonger, blind to local economic problems – unfairly, as he had argued in the Cabinet for measures to fight unemployment. Scrymgeour, the local Prohibitionist, and a Labour candidate were elected as the two MPs. The election was disastrous for both the Asquith and Lloyd George wings of the Liberal party, which together won fewer seats than Labour. Churchill took defeat philosophically. 'In the twinkling of an eye I found myself without an office, without a seat, and without an appendix', he quipped.

Financially, he was now better off due to an inheritance that allowed him to buy Chartwell Manor in Kent (see Chapter 7), which became his lifelong home. When Bonar Law fell ill and resigned in May 1923, Stanley Baldwin, always far friendlier to Churchill, became Conservative leader. Baldwin called a surprise election in November – but on a Protectionist programme Churchill could not accept. Churchill stood as a Liberal in Leicester and lost. The Conservatives lost too, Labour forming its first government with Liberal support. This dismayed Churchill, who still saw Labour as semi-Communist. In March 1924 he contested the seat of Westminster in a by-election as a 'Constitutionalist', losing narrowly to the Conservative candidate who had not, as he expected, stood down in his favour. When the Labour government fell in October 1924, Churchill again stood as a 'Constitutionalist' in Epping. This time the Conservatives did not oppose him and he decisively won the seat he was to hold for 40 years, soon as an open Conservative. His return to the Conservative fold – 're-ratting', as he put it – was less opportunistic than pragmatic, for the Liberals were now hopelessly divided between Asquith's and Lloyd George's followers. But such a return was predictable for, as commentator Ian Hamilton put it, 'the bedrock of this singular being is Conservatism'. His was, however, a highly individual form of conservatism.

To his surprised delight, Baldwin, now Prime Minister again, offered Churchill the Chancellorship of the Exchequer. He accepted the office his father once had with tears of gratitude; he had kept his father's old robes in camphor. The great financial issue of the time was: should Britain return to the pre-war Gold Standard? This meant an upward valuation of the currency, making exports more expensive and requiring a squeeze on British wages. Churchill, who never claimed to be a financial genius, called in the experts. Montagu Norman, Governor of the Bank of England, argued strongly for a return to the Gold Standard. The great economist Maynard Keynes argued against it. Churchill, finally swayed by the majority of bank opinion, announced the return to gold in his first Budget of April 1925. Other measures included cuts in naval expenditure – assuming that there would be no major war 'within the next 10 years', which especially affected the proposed naval base at Singapore – and pensions at 65 instead of 70.

The main result was the General Strike of 1926. Starting as a coal-miners' dispute – with which Churchill had some sympathy for miners were being asked to accept a cut in their already meagre wages to compete with cheaper foreign coal – it developed by May 1926 into a General Strike of all workers. Churchill, fighting instincts roused, quickly saw reddest Bolshevist revolution in this peaceful if potentially crippling dispute. He wanted to bring in the army and put tanks on the streets. Instead, the pacific Baldwin put him in charge of the *British Gazette*, the government newspaper published during the strike. Churchill edited this with customary zeal, supervising every detail and interfering with the typesetters, to make the paper a lively if biased read with a circulation of 2.5 million. When criticized for his partisan viewpoint, he replied, 'I decline utterly to be impartial between the fire brigade and the fire', although many considered his actions to be fanning rather than quenching the flames. The strike in fact ended peacefully after ten days, except for the coal miners' strike which dragged on damagingly. Churchill, with his usual magnanimity to the defeated, tried to broker a settlement but without success, for the mine owners now proved intransigent. Churchill's hot-headed speeches in the Strike confirmed his popular image as hostile to the working class.

Churchill's time at the Treasury was marked by a dashing, even buccaneer, approach to the nation's finances, in bad shape owing to trade depressions and the revalued pound. He increased road taxes, shortened brewers' credit (which gave the Treasury a temporary boost), increased duties on wine and spirits and decreased agricultural and business rates. More ambitious plans to reform the rating system were thwarted by Neville Chamberlain, Health Minister. *The Times* commented on his 'brilliantly entertaining … Budget speeches' and the young MP Harold Macmillan wrote that he 'brought a sense of colour into our rather drab political life'. But this did not save the Conservatives from electoral defeat in May 1929. Labour formed a government and Churchill was out of office. He was also to be out of favour, and deeply out fashion, for all the next decade.

7 Husband, Father, Painter, Writer

Through all the ups and downs of Churchill's life, he was sustained by an exceptionally happy marriage. When young, Churchill was shy with women of his age, partly because he was useless at dancing or light conversation, essential in Edwardian high society, partly because with little inherited money, he felt unable to contemplate marriage. Early romantic attachments, such as that to Muriel Wilson, daughter of a shipping magnate, came to nothing. But by 1908 he was both a successful writer and President of the Board of Trade. His younger brother Jack married that year, his mother had remarried years before, so he had no immediate family to supply a home. In 1904 he had briefly met Clementine Hozier but did not see her again until March 1908, when she was 23, nine years his junior. Clementine was the daughter of Sir Henry Hozier, a former soldier, writer and stockbroker, who had died in 1907, and Blanche, eldest daughter of the Earl of Airlie. Their marriage had not been a happy one and had broken up, leaving Blanche impoverished and Clementine without a proper education. Highly intelligent, beneath a conventional surface, Clementine was unusually independent in outlook, being a convinced Liberal and supporter of the suffragettes. But she was considered classically beautiful with a 'finished, flawless beauty' and had already turned down several suitors.

Churchill fell in love with her, although at first Clementine appeared indifferent to him. However, his remarkable bravery in August that year, when, heedless of danger, he helped save the contents of a house he was staying in that had caught fire – its roof collapsed seconds after he had rescued some statues – impressed her. So did his astonishing all-round energy and vision. He invited her to stay in Blenheim Palace that August. While they were sheltering from the rain in a summerhouse in the park, he proposed. They were married on 12 September at St Margaret's, Westminster. The invited guests numbered 1,400 while the streets outside were packed with onlookers. Churchill's best man was Lord David Cecil, but Lloyd George signed the registry as a witness, a significant pointer to the future dominance of politics in their lives. When honeymooning in Venice, Churchill insisted on taking motorboats rather than gondolas because they were quicker, and wrote numerous official letters. Clementine must have realized very early that work was her husband's overwhelming priority in life.

But Churchill *had* married for love – rather than money or influence as was often the case – and the marriage turned out a great success, at least for him. In his words, he 'married and lived happily ever afterwards'. They called each other Pug and Kat; Churchill, returning home in the evening, would bark up the stairs and Clementine would miaow back to him. Her common sense and humanity balanced his impetuous egotism and extravagance, although some politicians, such as Asquith, found her dull. When Churchill shouted her down in arguments, she did not answer directly but sent him reasoned notes, fearlessly reprimanding him for what she saw as his wrong behaviour – for example, towards his colleagues after he first became Prime Minister in 1940. Churchill normally took this in good part, and he relied completely on her support and fidelity. The latter was only once challenged, when Clementine went on a cruise by herself in 1935 and met Terence Philip, a handsome art dealer with whom she fell in love. Nothing, however, came of it. Churchill himself seems hardly to have looked at another woman after marriage.

In 1909 the Churchills took a lease on a house in Eccleston Square, near Victoria Station, where two rooms became his library, and they entertained important persons of many types – not only Liberals but people of all parties. Their first child Diana was born there in July 1909, their second Randolph in May 1911. Their second daughter Sarah was born in October 1914. When Churchill celebrated his thirty-fifth birthday, Lord Esher, a guest, commented, 'He had a birthday cake with 35 candles. And *crackers!* ... He and she sat on the same sofa, and he holds her hand. I never saw two people more in love.' Their fourth child, Marigold, was born in November 1918 but lived less than three years, dying of septicaemia, to her parents' great grief. Clementine's last child Mary was born in September 1922.

When Churchill, thanks to a timely legacy from a distant relative in Ireland, bought Chartwell Manor near Westerham in Kent in 1922, it became the chief family home. Dating back to about 1500, Chartwell had been much altered by the Victorians and was riddled with rot, but it had stunning views over the Kentish Weald, the 'Garden of England', and a 300-acre estate whose potential Churchill at once set about realizing. He built a new four-storey wing facing south, had ponds, waterfalls and lakes dug out and dammed a stream, built a garden cottage and many brick walls, the last with his own hands. He publicized this manual feat by accepting an invitation to join the Building Workers Trade Union after checking that it did not restrict the number of bricks he could lay in a day. (He claimed normally to manage 200 bricks and 2,000 words on his books.) Numerous french windows connected the house and gardens.

The Churchills formally moved in 1924, after Churchill had spent £18,000 on improvements. The house had only cost £5,000 originally. Clementine supervized a full-scale replanting of the estate and tried to make the house as comfortable as possible, although the constant flow of visitors – some of whom she disliked – disrupted normal family life. Foremost among her unloved guests was Brendan Brackan, an Irish-born financier, newspaperman and MP, who became such a close follower and crony of Churchill's in the 1920s that it was rumoured he was Churchill's illegitimate son, a rumour Churchill found rather amusing. Brackan certainly shared his mentor's taste for heavy drinking, racy anecdotes and epithets, such as calling the immensely proper Lord Halifax 'Baldwin's bugger-boy'. Along with Professor Lindemann, Churchill's favourite 'boffin' or scientist – who kept Churchill up-to-date on technical matters but was a raging snob and reputedly Oxford's least popular don – they would stay up late at night, drinking, smoking and talking.

Unlike his own coldly distant father, however, Churchill loved his children, being an affectionate and indulgent parent, as far as his other commitments permitted. He enjoyed playing with them – he was particularly good at 'gorillas', in which he imitated a gorilla, trying to catch his children – and building them tree houses in the gardens at Chartwell. He gave Randolph, his only son, a choice of Eton or Harrow; significantly Randolph, after visiting both, chose the former because it had 'fewer rules and less discipline'. He was nonetheless caned there for being 'bloody awful all round'. The children began to accompany their parents on their frequent travels abroad, and in 1927 Randolph went with his father on a grand tour that included a call on the Pope and on Mussolini. By then the teenage Randolph was encouraged to stay up late night listening to, often arguing with, his father's important friends. Unfortunately, such evenings were lavishly fuelled by port and brandy. By the age of 18, Randolph was knocking back double brandies and by his twenties he was already an alcoholic, frequently in clinics to 'dry out'. He left Oxford without taking a degree to become a not very successful journalist, at one stage flirting with Oswald Mosley's Fascists. Twice in the 1930s he stood for Parliament as an independent without his father's foreknowledge but to his great embarrassment (see Chapter 8).

Diana, the eldest child, was also a heavy drinker. In 1932 she married John Bailey, son of a South African magnate, but the marriage, which her parents had opposed, did not last. In 1935 she married Duncan Sandys, one of the very few MPs who supported Churchill in the 1930s, but that marriage too failed and she committed suicide in 1963. Sarah, the third child, wanted a theatrical career – still considered unrespectable – and in 1935, while a chorus girl, she fell in love with Vic Oliver, an Australian comedian twice divorced and 17 years her senior. They were married in New York in 1936 amid extensive adverse publicity. Only Mary, devoted to country pursuits, supported rather than undermined her parents, finally marrying Christopher Soames, a captain in the Coldstream Guards.

Among Churchill's many other pursuits – polo, golf, fox-hunting, gambling – one provided special balm: painting. He was introduced to it in 1915, at the height of the Dardanelles disaster, by his sister-in-law Gwendoline and took to it with his usual enthusiasm, buying up 'the entire contents of Robertson's colour-shop in Piccadilly – easels, palettes, brushes, tubes and canvases'. Painting was the one activity which so entirely occupied him that he was totally silent as he worked, cigar in mouth, panama hat on head. Although not good at drawing, his landscapes brim with rich colour dramatically employed. Soon he was taking his paintbox with him on his travels, often painting two canvases a day. He was inspired especially by the Mediterranean's brilliant light, adopting Pointillist techniques to capture it. Later, some of his landscapes were exhibited at the Royal Academy's summer shows and in 1948 he was elected Honorary Academician Extraordinary. Typically, he persuaded Alfrend Munnings, then President of the RA, to revive its annual dinner.

If Churchill was an amateur painter, he was a highly professional writer. His first books concerning his own exploits were essentially journalistic and his one, typically romantic novel, *Romola*, was decidedly amateurish, but with the publication of his biography of Lord Randolph in 1906 he began to establish himself as a historian. Only after World War I did he have both the time and need to write full-time – he was out of Parliament from 1922 to 1924, with a growing family. He started his four-volume work on the Great War, *The World Crisis*, while still in Lloyd George's cabinet, completing the last volume in 1929. The books were widely reviewed and eagerly read, for they contained much topical information about the inner workings of government. Churchill was criticized for this disclosure by some politicians but was far more strongly attacked by generals, for he put the blame for the appalling 'war of attrition', which had claimed millions of lives, on their shoulders. He was not, of course, writing disinterestedly, and a counter-volume, *The World Crisis: A Criticism*, appeared in 1927 with hostile essays by several generals. But generally posterity has agreed more with Churchill than with them. As the *Manchester Guardian* put it, 'he cannot be dull in writing any more than in action'. The books proved very profitable, Churchill earning a £4,000 advance on the first volume and royalties of 33 per cent.

During the 1930s, his wilderness years, Churchill almost became a full-time writer. His autobiography *My Early Life* was published in 1930, detailing his life before he married. (This was just before he was run over by a car while crossing Fifth Avenue in New York. Fortunately, no bones were broken in the accident and he recovered remarkably rapidly, although his lecture tour had to be postponed.) Churchill later called this humorous, remarkably non-egotistical book 'the best … I ever wrote' and many have since agreed. But his chief literary concern in the 1930s was the monumental life of his ancestor, the first Duke of Marlborough. Churchill planned this as a rebuttal of the Victorian historian Macaulay's portrait of the Duke as a scheming miser. He visited Blenheim, Ramillies and Oudenarde, scenes of the Duke's great victories; sent researchers to scour the archives in Vienna and Paris as well as Blenheim and London; he employed a military expert, Colonel Packenham-Walsh to check military details and draw maps. The first volume, lavishly illustrated, came out in 1933, the last of the four in 1938, making a total of about one million words. If some felt that he attacked Macaulay too much, and painted his often grasping and disloyal ancestor as an unblemished 'virtuous and benevolent being', there was a general enthusiasm for a work that excelled at military descriptions. 'Too much history is written by don-bred dons', wrote Professor Lewis Namier approvingly. Prophetically, the critic Desmond MacCarthy praised its 'educative value for anyone who proposes to take a hand in national affairs or may some day find himself in a position of public responsibility'.

Churchill then turned to an even bigger task, his *History of the English-Speaking Peoples.* This grandiose project was primarily a pot-boiler, earning an advance of £20,000, but was also intended to strengthen ties between Britain and America. Starting with Roman Britain, it marched majestically through the centuries, and by 1939 nearly 500,000 words had been written, when war intervened. It was not completed until the late 1950s. Thanks also to numerous articles he wrote for papers in the US and Britain, Churchill was earning about £20,000 a year from his writings by the mid-1930s (perhaps £600,000 today). After 1945, again out of office, he started writing his six-volume *History of the Second War* for both American and British publishers. Uniquely well-qualified as he was to write it, this history, although highly partial and often verbose, has helped mould the way that conflict has since been viewed.

Such titanic literary labours were only possible, even for a man as energetic as Churchill, because he did not actually write, let alone research, his books. Instead, he relied on paid researchers whose findings he absorbed into his general framework and dictated whole pages to his secretaries, striding up and down. Proofs were then sent out to several people to read, their comments being incorporated at this stage. Although he tried very hard to be accurate, he never let 'the facts get in the way of the phrases' as he impishly put it, loving to embellish his rich prose with pungent phrases. His approach was not that of an analytic academic but of a grand storyteller, and his histories were tales of great men – generals, aristocrats, ministers – not of ordinary working people, nor even of famous poets or scientists. This attitude has been attacked by academics like J. H. Plumb as 'old Whig claptrap', meaning that it envisions English history as moving along grand and inevitable avenues. But it was part of Churchill's romantic approach to all life and his books remain very readable, although their high-flown rhetoric now seems Victorian. In recognition of his unique output, Churchill was awarded the Nobel Prize for Literature in 1953.

8 The Wilderness Years

Churchill left office shortly before the onset of the Great Depression, which, with the rise of Nazism, was to dominate politics in the coming decade. If half-ignored as an ex-minister at home, he had tremendous success on a lecture tour across Canada and the US. Returning via New York, he unwisely invested much of his earnings in the stock market just before it crashed in October 1929. His frantic writing efforts over the next decade were partly an attempt to recoup by the pen what he had lost on the market. He was without a minister's salary just when his children, especially his son Randolph, were beginning to emulate his extravagant lifestyle. This long period out of office was due not to the Conservatives being out of power – from 1931 they dominated the 'National' coalition government – but to his repeated disagreements with Baldwin, the Tory leader. Baldwin, pipe-smoking and reassuringly peaceful, embodied the national mood of 'safety first', which meant retrenchment at home and appeasement abroad, both attitudes totally alien to Churchill.

Their first disagreement, however, was over tariff reform. Lord Beaverbrook, the newspaper magnate, threw his papers' weight behind a campaign to impose tariffs on all non-Empire goods. The issue had resurfaced due to the Great Depression, which was proving beyond the competence of Ramsay Macdonald's Labour government. If protectionist proposals were still anathema to Churchill, Baldwin proved ready to listen, if not to agree, especially when Beaverbrook put up 'Empire Crusade' candidates to oppose Conservatives in by-elections. In January 1931, Churchill finally quit the Shadow Cabinet. By then another, much greater area of disagreement had emerged.

In 1917, Lloyd George's wartime government had promised India that it would ultimately have dominion status, i.e. near independence within the Empire, like Australia or Canada. Successive post-war governments had prevaricated on this promise, enraging many Indians who began a programme of civil disobedience led by Gandhi. In October 1929, the Viceroy (governor) of India, Lord Irwin, later Lord Halifax, restated the goal of dominion status and announced a Round Table Conference to which the leaders of the Indian Congress would be invited. Churchill loudly cheered Lloyd George's speech deploring this in the Commons, and soon found himself attacking the whole concept in articles and speeches with his usual pungency. He warned of 'a Hindu despotism or a renewal of … ferocious internal wars' and that 'Gandhism … will, sooner or later, have to be grappled with and finally crushed. It is no use trying to satisfy a tiger by feeding him with cat's-meat'. Such provocative statements made him popular with the India Defence League, formed to defend the imperial status quo, especially when he famously described Gandhi as a 'seditious Middle Temple lawyer, now posing as a fakir of a type well-known in the East, striding half-naked up the steps of the Viceregal palace'. But they did him no good in the corridors of power.

As Baldwin was considering joining a coalition under Ramsay Macdonald, the stumbling Labour leader, Churchill was damning himself politically. Some saw his speeches as an attempt to build his own power basis to challenge Baldwin but Churchill was too straightforward, indeed naive, for such manoeuvres. He feared for the future of India's minorities, especially its Muslims and Untouchables, and genuinely thought the subcontinent was not ready for dominion status. However, he had not visited India for over 30 years and was no expert on its current state, still admiring its rajahs and maharajahs. In his rejection of Irwin's proposals he voiced what many right-wing Conservative MPs secretly felt but few said. But while Churchill spoke wildly of splitting the Tory party over India, only about 40 MPs ever voted with him against the government on the issue. The National (coalition) government had, since the General Election of 1931, an overwhelming majority, with 554 seats in the Commons.

Churchill, swallowing his Free Trade convictions, comfortably retained his Epping seat at this election, but if still in Parliament, he had little influence on what went on there and at times seemed to have little interest. He now appeared in the House only occasionally, usually when he himself wanted to speak, and ostentatiously ignored other MPs' speeches, yawning or fidgeting. Such boorishness was particularly resented during new MPs' maiden speeches, traditionally heard with courtesy. He declined to take part in the Select Parliamentary Committee examining the Indian question, giving the impression that he was opposed to *any* reforms. Above all, his language, describing the pacifistic Gandhi as an 'evil and malignant Brahmin' probably in German pay, and his repeated cries 'Wake up, England!' sounded absurdly alarmist. His position was not helped when his son Randolph, without telling him beforehand, stood as an Independent against the National government at a by-election in January 1935. Churchill loyally spoke in Randolph's favour, resulting in a split vote giving the seat to Labour. That year the Government of India Act was passed despite all his warnings.

The tragedy of his mistaken stance over India was that his truly prophetic warnings over Nazi Germany fell for long on deaf ears. Hitler began secretly rearming soon after coming to power in Germany in January 1933 and Churchill at once began to grow alarmed. In March 1933 he spoke of 'the tumultuous insurgency of ferocity and war spirit, the pitiless ill-treatment of minorities' in Germany. He clearly understood Hitler from the start despite the Führer's constant protestations of peace. But few other people in Britain did, and when Churchill publicly thanked God for the French army, still the biggest in Europe, most people grimaced rather than agreed. Any mention of war was still anathema. The Oxford Union, the university's famous debating society, passed a motion saying they would not fight for 'King and Country', which was much publicized abroad. Churchill warned particularly of the threat posed by the growing Luftwaffe (German air force) to Britain, painting lurid pictures of London destroyed by German fire bombs and gas, hundreds of thousands killed and millions more in panic fleeing into the countryside. He predicted – inaccurately – that the Luftwaffe would overtake the RAF by the end of 1935. Baldwin played down such fears until Hitler told the Foreign Secretary visiting Berlin in March 1935 that the Luftwaffe had *already* achieved parity with the RAF. This was not yet true but it forced Baldwin, who became Prime Minister in June, to double the RAF's budget. It also led him to invite Churchill to join the Air Defence Research Committee 'as a gesture of friendliness to an old colleague'. This was small compensation for not being given a Cabinet post, but Churchill could at least learn of, and even influence, developments in the RAF.

Churchill's problem throughout the 1930s was that he was distrusted by the pacifist-inclined left in general, who shared his abhorrence of the Nazis but called for collective action through the League of Nations, but he was also alienated from most Conservatives. Churchill himself had little time for the League of Nations. In 1935 Mussolini, the Fascist dictator of Italy, invaded Abyssinia (Ethiopia), a blatant act of aggression condemned by the League. Britain imposed half-hearted sanctions that failed to deter Mussolini. The British and French foreign ministers, respectively Hoare and Laval, then drew up a plan ceding most of Abyssinia to Mussolini. Such a surrender provoked an uproar and both ministers had to resign in December. Anthony Eden replaced Hoare, attempting to breathe new vigour into the League. Churchill, who might have been expected to oppose the surrender, was away in France painting at the time and said little on his return. This was partly because he half-admired Mussolini, in whom he saw a Napoleonic figure – he hero-worshipped Napoleon – and a potential ally against Germany, while despising Abyssinia for its backwardness. As it turned out, Mussolini joined Hitler in the 'Axis', soon being drawn along in Hitler's wake.

Earlier in 1933, Churchill had been indifferent to Chinese appeals to the League for help against Japanese aggression in Manchuria. He felt that China was utterly corrupt and the Japanese posed no real threat to British interests, a view he maintained up to their attack on Pearl Harbor in 1941. Nor did he speak out against Franco and the Fascists when they launched the Spanish Civil War in July 1936, seeing them as a lesser evil to the loathed Reds, who predominated in the Republican government. If such actions ruined his hopes with the Left, his warnings against Hitler did not impress most right-wing Conservative MPs, who saw Nazism as a bulwark against Communism.

When Hitler's troops in March 1936 marched into the Rhineland, which Germany had been bound by treaty to leave 'demilitarized', Baldwin rejected tentative French proposals to repel them. With hindsight this would have been easy – German army orders were to retreat if the French even moved – and Churchill spoke derisively of 'funk versus national honour'. But most people in Britain supported Baldwin, who dismissed it just as Hitler marching 'into his own backyard'. Even so, Churchill's relations with Baldwin improved that summer until the Abdication Crisis. Edward VIII, who had become King in January 1936, wanted desperately to marry Mrs Simpson, an American divorcée. Baldwin and the establishment regarded her as totally unsuitable and tried hard to dissuade the King. Edward, however, was determined, and the crisis, carefully hidden from the British public, deepened in the autumn. Finally, in December, the King decided to abdicate 'to marry the woman he loved'.

Churchill, quixotically loyal to a monarch he did not know well, called in the Commons on 7 December for a pause before doing anything irrevocable immediately after Baldwin had spoken to universal applause. Churchill's speech was howled down and he seemed finished as a politician, his personal support in the Commons reduced to just his son-in-law Duncan Sandys and Brendan Brackan, his closest companion. Neville Chamberlain, who replaced Baldwin as Prime Minister in 1937, distrusted Churchill and proved even keener on appeasing the Axis dictators, Hitler and Mussolini. In March 1938, Germany annexed Austria in the *Anschluss*, which meant that Czechoslovakia, with its large German minority, was surrounded by Nazi territory. Hitler began to press the Czechs to hand over the Sudetenland, the area ringing their country, dwelling on the (largely imaginary) sufferings of Germans living there under Czech rule. Chamberlain, determined at any cost to avert war, was content to see Czechoslovakia dismembered and flew to Germany to meet Hitler three times. On the third occasion in Munich on 28 September 1938, Chamberlain agreed to hand over much of Czechoslovakia, in return for a piece of paper on which Hitler promised peace. Returning to Britain, he was cheered in the streets and in the House of Commons for bringing 'peace in our time'.

Churchill was not alone in condemning this surrender but he was far the most eloquent, standing out like a rock against the flow of appeasers. 'We have suffered a total and unmitigated defeat', he warned the Commons, to deafening cries of protest. 'We have sustained a defeat without war, the consequences of which will travel far with us along our road … Do not suppose that this is the end. This is only the beginning of the reckoning … the first foretaste of a bitter cup which will be proffered to us year by year unless … we arise again and take our stand for freedom as in the olden time.' His sombre warnings found few listeners that autumn.

If Churchill had died at the end of 1938, he would have been considered, like his father, a failure after a brilliant early career. But he lived on, to be gloriously vindicated. In March 1939, Hitler's troops occupied the rest of Czechoslovakia, which was solidly Czech, with no German-speakers except in Prague, where many were Jewish. Chamberlain's peace treaty was shown to be totally worthless and the British began to accept that war was inevitable if Hitler was ever to be stopped. That spring and summer, Hitler put pressure on Poland, his next victim, which also had a large German minority and whose sovereignty Chamberlain had rashly guaranteed. In England, pressure now began to grow to include Churchill in the government, but few yet saw him as a possible Prime Minister. When Germany invaded Poland on 1 September 1939, Britain and France issued an ultimatum to Germany which lapsed on 3 September. World War II had begun. Unwillingly, Chamberlain offered Churchill his old post as First Lord of the Admiralty, which he happily accepted. The message flashed round the navy: 'Winston is back.'

9 The Finest Hours

Returning to the Admiralty after 24 years, Churchill found many things the same, although 'an entirely different generation filled the uniforms and the posts'. But the Royal Navy, although its relative superiority had increased over the Germans numerically, was no longer a thoroughly modern force. Most battleships dated from the previous war and lacked adequate anti-aircraft defences. Churchill at first underestimated the threat posed by both aircraft and submarines to surface vessels.

Although turning 65, he amazed the navy by his energy – fuelled by whisky because his doctor had ordered him 'to take nothing non-alcoholic between breakfast and dinner' – staying up late every night to pore over charts. The energy with which he mobilized the fleet impressed the public, who did not blame him for the loss of the battleship Royal Oak, torpedoed at anchor in Scapa Flow in the Orkneys with heavy losses in October. Churchill could take credit for the sinking of several U-boats – although their numbers were exaggerated – and for the Battle of the River Plate in December. This was the clash between the German 'pocket battleship' *Graf Spee* – pocket because it was built unusually small for its armaments, to comply with the Versailles Peace Treaty's restrictions – and three light British cruisers. The *Graf Spee*'s far heavier guns should have given it victory but it was chased into neutral Montevideo harbour. Obeying Hitler's enraged orders, its captain then sailed out and scuttled it, committing suicide. Churchill increased the production of small frigates to counter the U-boat menace, which he foresaw increasing, at the expense of building more battleships, but was slow to accept that a full convoy system was the only way to protect merchant shipping from U-boat attack. Instead, he wanted destroyers to act in 'hunter-killer' groups against U-boats.

The winter of 1939–40 saw the 'Phoney War', with no land fighting between Germany and the allies, France and Britain. However, Stalin attacked Finland in November to gain strategically important territory. The Russians at first did remarkably badly and Churchill, longing to help the Finns, wanted to send a fleet into the Baltic – without air cover. Such impracticable ideas were foiled by wiser counsel in the navy and Cabinet, but a ship ventured into neutral Norway's waters to free British prisoners on the German ship *Altmark*. Churchill also proposed laying mines round Norway to cut off Germany's iron ore supplies from Sweden. Hitler, however, ended Norway's neutrality on 8 April 1940, over-running Denmark and southern Norway. Further north, the Norwegians fought back, and the allies decided to help with troops and ships. Despite isolated successes, such as the sinking of eight German destroyers in Narvik Fjord, British forces failed to stop the Germans seizing the key ports and by the end of April the troops had to be evacuated, some being taken prisoner. The Norwegian campaign revealed alarmingly that German air superiority more than offset British superiority at sea.

Defeat in Norway led to a political crisis at home. Churchill, recently appointed head of the Military Co-ordination Committee, (half-way to being Minister of Defence), defended the government in the Commons on 8 May. Speaking for many, the Conservative Leopold Amery called out to Chamberlain, 'In the name of God, go!' Chamberlain realized that he must resign, but wanted Lord Halifax, his foreign secretary, to succeed him. At a fateful meeting on 9 May, Churchill remained unusually silent when this was suggested. Halifax said being a peer would make his premiership difficult and Churchill 'with suitable expressions of regard and humility', agreed, so becoming Prime Minister almost by default. Only a year before he had been out of office, but he now 'felt as if I were walking with Destiny, and that all my past life had been but a preparation for this hour and this trial'.

The trial began immediately, for Hitler invaded (neutral) Holland and Belgium on 10 May ending the 'Phoney War'. Chamberlain tried to retain power in the new crisis but Labour refused to serve under him and Churchill was accepted as Prime Minister – without enthusiasm by most Conservatives. He formed a coalition government, bringing in Clement Attlee, Herbert Morrison and others from Labour and Archibald Sinclair from the Liberals, and soon making Beaverbrook Minister of Munitions. He made himself Minister of Defence, a controversial appointment he fully justified.

On 13 May, Churchill made his first great speech to the Commons as Prime Minister. 'I have nothing to offer but blood, toil, tears and sweat', he declared, continuing, 'You ask: What is our policy? I will say: it is to wage war, by sea, land and air, with all our might and with all the strength that God can give us; to wage war against a monstrous tyranny, never surpassed in the dark, lamentable catalogue of human crime. That is our policy. You ask: What is our aim? I answer in one word. It is Victory: victory at all costs, victory in spite of all terror, victory, however long and hard the road may be, for without victory there is no survival.' Amid cheers, the new ministry was approved by 381 votes to none.

Confident and vigorous, Churchill moved into No 10 Downing Street with Brendan Bracken and Professor Lindemann, his scientific adviser. 'Within a fortnight all was changed … a sense of urgency was created in the course of a very few days and respectable civil servants were actually to be seen running along their corridors', recalled Jock Colville, his secretary. Although some stuffier people like Lord Reith, former head of the BBC, detested Churchill's 'monstrous obstinacy and wrong-headedness', most realized that he was quintessentially the right man for the crisis. The German *Blitzkrieg* (lightning war) was proving unstoppable, overwhelming Holland and Belgium. On 15 May the French Premier Reynaud telephoned to announce: 'We have been defeated … we have lost the battle', as German panzers broke through at Sedan and drove for the Channel. To rally the French, Churchill flew to France three times in the next month, at considerable personal risk. Reynaud begged him to send over the remaining RAF fighter squadrons, earmarked for Britain's own defence, but Churchill prevaricated, especially after a counter-offensive against the German flank failed due to the French army's collapse. This failure left the British army trapped perilously against the Channel coast.

The victorious evacuation from the Dunkirk beaches followed. In just nine days from 26 May an armada of small boats – including yachts, pleasure steamers and fishing boats – brought back 338,000 troops, a quarter of them French, without heavy equipment but most with their rifles. The British army lived on to fight again. On 4 June, however, Churchill reminded the Commons: 'Wars are not won by evacuations.' He went on to declare: 'We shall fight on the beaches, we shall fight on the landing-grounds, we shall fight in the hills; we shall never surrender and even if, which I do not for a moment believe, this island or a large part of it were subjugated and starving, then our Empire beyond the seas, armed and guarded by the British Fleet, would carry on the struggle until, in God's good time the New World with all its power and might steps forth to the rescue and liberation of the Old.' Such tremendous eloquence, however, could not affect events in France. The French government fled from Paris and on 25 June capitulated to the Germans, handing over northern and western France while moving to Vichy.

Britain's situation appeared desperate. Germany controlled the Atlantic coast from the North Cape (Norway) to the Pyrenees (France), giving its submarines and aircraft wonderful bases to attack Britain; the Italians, who had entered the war on 10 June, threatened links with the Middle East; the Luftwaffe looked invincible and the German army was vastly stronger than the British, although the Royal Navy was much superior to the German. Far from despairing, Churchill seemed exhilarated by the prospect. Dismissing ideas of peace negotiations after a brief Cabinet discussion – in which Halifax still hoped that Mussolini might act as a mediator – he rallied the nation with some of the greatest political speeches ever made. What had often been a liability to him in peacetime – his old-fashioned rhetoric, his indomitable bellicosity, his impish sense of humour and his flamboyance typified by his perpetual cigar and odd costumes – now matched the nation's need perfectly. On 18 June he warned, 'The Battle of France is over. I expect that the Battle of Britain is about to begin ... Let us therefore brace ourselves to our duties, and so bear ourselves that, if the British Empire and its Commonwealth last for a thousand years, men will still say: "This was their finest hour".' Soon his broadcast speeches were being eagerly awaited by the nation.

The Battle of Britain, the struggle for air control over southern England crucial if Germany was to invade successfully, began in late July. Britain had one big advantage in its radar network, only recently completed, whose powers of distant detection the Germans long failed to recognize adequately. But the Luftwaffe, although it had more bombers in 1940 than the RAF, did not have more fighters, thanks to the efforts of Beaverbrook, Munitions Minister, who increased the number of Hurricanes and Spitfires in service from 331 after Dunkirk to 620, with 289 in reserve, by early August. (In 1940 Britain produced more aircraft than Germany.) The Home Guard numbered a million men by July and the regular army, re-equipped with rifles and artillery bought from the US, was fortifying the south and east coasts with pillboxes and anti-tank ditches. They were never needed as the Luftwaffe failed to crush the RAF. The climax of the air battle came on 15 September. The RAF threw in its last fighter reserves just as the German bombers turned for home, a process watched by Churchill from Fighter Headquarters at Uxbridge. The Luftwaffe, losing 53 aircraft that day, switched its attacks from well-defended airfields and radar stations to bombing London, soon restricting even this to less costly night attacks. Two days later Sea Lion, German codename for invading Britain, was indefinitely postponed. 'Never in the field of human conflict was so much owed by so many to so few', Churchill said of the fighter pilots. Broadcasting to the French in his inimitable French on 21 October, he could afford to joke: 'Nous attendons l'invasion promise de longue date; aussi les poissons.' ('We are waiting for the long-promised invasion. So are the fishes.').

The 'Blitz' that followed was meant to break Britain's spirit and cripple its industrial output by repeated night bombing. It did neither, for air-raid precautions mitigated the worst effects. Churchill encouraged the use of the London Tube as a giant bomb shelter – overruling civil servants – and shared Londoners' dangers by staying in Westminster throughout the week, often watching the night battle from an observation post near No 10. Already he was very popular, opinion polls showing that over 80 per cent approved his handling of the war, a figure that hardly dropped in coming years. When he visited the London Docks in September after a raid, he was moved to tears by people's undaunted enthusiasm. 'Good old Winnie', they cried. 'We thought you'd come and see us. We can take it. Give it 'em back!'

Churchill took one major precaution: the House of Commons now sat in the day, rather than at night, because, as he put it: 'We ought not to imagine we are irreplaceable but it cannot be denied that two or three hundred by-elections would be a quite needless complication of our affairs.' Soon the Luftwaffe turned to attacking other cities, especially Coventry, whose cathedral was destroyed on 14 November, but although it caused great damage, the Blitz was foiled. Churchill toured the bomb-damaged cities keeping up morale with his V-signs – an outward-handed gesture for Victory, although Churchill knew perfectly well what it could also mean – and his own perennially cheering presence. 'Are we down-hearted?' he shouted at a crowd at the gates of a north-east England shipyard. 'No!' they replied with a roar. Churchill, for all his patrician background, had far more of the 'common touch' than most civil servants or politicians. He renamed the Local Defence Volunteers the 'Home Guard', for instance, and Communal Feeding Centres 'British Restaurants', reasoning that 'restaurant' at least *implies* a good meal.

Churchill soon evolved his wartime routine: rising late after working on papers in bed, drinking a bottle of champagne in the morning and many other drinks later, taking a siesta after 'a most lavish' lunch but working late into the night. He thrived on such a regime, seldom seeming affected by drink, looking rosy-cheeked and years younger than in the 1930s. However, secretaries and assistants, deprived of weekends, holidays or even sleep, often flagged. 'We must go on like gun-horses till we drop', he told one secretary exhausted after hours of dictation. Despite such demands and bouts of bad temper, his staff generally loved him. His generals and admirals had more mixed feelings, often being taunted as cowards when they (correctly) pointed out the risks of his numerous madder projects. General Alan Brooke, the dour but omnicompetent Chief of Imperial General Staff who always refused to be browbeaten, later recalled 'unbounded genius, unrelenting energy, dogged determination, a refusal to accept defeat … a deep sense of humour and an uncanny faculty for inspiring respect, admiration, loyalty and deep affection'. His posthumously published diaries reveal his frequent annoyance, however.

Never happy on the defensive, Churchill determined to strike back in the Mediterranean, where Mussolini's troops threatened Egypt from Libya. He sent out most of Britain's tanks during the Battle of Britain – a seemingly rash act justified by events. The first British attack, however, was on the French fleet stationed in Mediterranean ports, where it tempted the Axis powers. In July 1940 Churchill ordered it seized – or, if that proved impossible as it did at Oran, Algeria, sunk, a bitter action against an ex-ally. An attempt to land General de Gaulle, leader of the Free French, in Dakar, French West Africa, proved an embarrassing fiasco in September, as its Vichy French troops resisted. More pleasing was the repulsion of Mussolini's invasion of Egypt. In December British troops under Wavell drove the Italians out of Egypt and captured half of Libya, taking 113,00 prisoners. Italy's battle-fleet was crippled by an air attack on Taranto in November. Churchill now began pressing Wavell to intervene against Axis sympathizers in Syria and Iraq, and to help Greece, which Mussolini had also attacked. Wavell, short of men, demurred, provoking Churchill's wrath. But when the Germans, helping their Italian allies, swept into Greece in April 1941, British Commonwealth troops were sent in. The campaign proved a disaster, the British, Australians and New Zealanders being driven back to Crete, which they had to evacuate in the face of airborne invasion. Meanwhile General Rommel and his Afrika Korps had consolidated earlier victories in Libya. When Wavell, prodded by Churchill, attacked Rommel in June, he was heavily defeated. Churchill replaced him with Auchinleck, whom he soon berated too for lack of offensive spirit. Churchill would never take 'Not Ready' for an answer.

Such military action taxed Britain's strength and Churchill began begging US President Roosevelt for aid. Britain was running out of foreign currency for vital imports, but US law demanded cash for arms. In August 1940 Roosevelt had given Britain 50 obsolete destroyers in return for military bases in the British empire. After winning re-election in November he persuaded Congress in March 1941 to pass the Lend-Lease Bill, which allowed Britain – and later Greece, China and Russia – to draw on almost limitless American government credit for weapons. Churchill called this 'the most unsordid act in the history of the world' for it meant that the industrial might of the US could now be turned against Germany. 'Give us the tools and we will finish the job', he quipped. Uniquely qualified through his background to cultivate Anglo-American relations, he crossed over in person to meet Roosevelt at Placentia Bay, Newfoundland, in August 1941, hoping to persuade the president to declare war. Instead, they drew up the 'Atlantic Charter' of democratic ideals. The two leaders became friends but the US would not enter the war, although American destroyers began escorting British convoys as far as Iceland.

Instead, Hitler attacked Russia on 22 June 1941, catching it completely unprepared. Churchill, hearing of German plans in April, had alerted Stalin, but the Soviet dictator ignored all warnings. When asked how he would react to this invasion, Churchill joked: 'If Hitler invaded Hell, I would at least make a favourable reference to the Devil in the House of Commons.' He did far more, however, drawing up an official alliance in July and diverting American aid to Russia, perilously transported by British convoys to Murmansk. The speed of the German advance –

they reached Smolensk, over half-way to Moscow, in six weeks – dismayed many, including even Churchill, with his long historical imagination. Britain's own position was still grim. Auchinleck's offensive in north Africa in November achieved little against Rommel's superior tanks; Malta, lynchpin of Britain's Mediterranean defence, was threatened and the 'Battle of the North Atlantic' as Churchill termed the crucial fight against German U-boats (submarines) was not going well. Then, on 7 December, came news of the surprise Japanese attack on the American fleet at Pearl Harbor. Three days later Hitler declared war on the US. Churchill was jubilant. 'So we had won after all', he wrote later.

The Grand Alliance 10

If Churchill rejoiced at Pearl Harbor and its likely consequences, so did Adolf Hitler, who thought Japan invincible. In the short run, events seemed to prove Hitler right, for the Japanese, after crippling the main US fleet in Pearl Harbor, swept across the Pacific and South-east Asia. Singapore, the huge British base intended to safeguard Australia and New Zealand, was very vulnerable as the Japanese marched into Thailand, which allied with them. This vulnerability was partly Churchill's fault, for he had belittled possible Japanese threats since the time when, as Chancellor, he had slashed expenditure on Singapore's fortifications. By 1941 Singapore boasted defences only against *naval* attacks, and the Japanese came by land. Churchill had sent out two modern battleships, the *Prince of Wales* and the *Renown*, in late 1941, but the aircraft-carrier accompanying them ran aground and they reached Far Eastern waters unprotected. Sailing to shell Japanese troops landing in north Malaya on 10 December, they were both sunk by Japanese aircraft. The subsequent fall of Malaya led to that of Singapore on 15 February 1942, with the capture of 60,000 British and Australian troops, most of whom had not fired a shot. This, the greatest British military disaster since the Dardanelles, let the Japanese swiftly conquer the Dutch East Indies (Indonesia) and Burma, pressing up against India. Australia and much of Asia seemed within their grasp.

'What sort of people do they [the Japanese] think we are?' Churchill asked indignantly, speaking to the assembled Houses of Congress in Washington on 26 December, a rare honour for a foreigner. His speech ended by his declaring, 'In days to come the British and American peoples will … for the good of all walk together side by side in majesty, in justice and peace', receiving a standing ovation. He had spent Christmas with Roosevelt in the White House, helping light the Christmas tree. Churchill suffered a minor heart attack soon after and, after seeing in the New Year in Washington, went south to recuperate in Florida. However, he recovered fully and rapidly, even piloting the flying-boat part of his way home. Transatlantic flights were still quite risky, but Churchill loved flying.

Although worried by events in Asia and the Pacific, Churchill was convinced that defeating Germany must come first. Roosevelt, ignoring those admirals who favoured the Pacific, agreed. Churchill now worked to cement the Grand Alliance of the US, Britain and Soviet Russia, an awkward combination of allies with different political systems and aims. Relations with the US were paramount, helped by the personal rapport between Roosevelt and Churchill. Britain, even with its still vast Commonwealth and Empire, was much the smallest of the 'Big Three', as increasingly became apparent. Churchill gradually found that he was no longer the master of events, but merely one among several important political and military figures. However, he naively hoped that American power would help restore Britain's imperial position after the war, while the US actually wanted to dissolve the British empire.

The issue of the Second Front, an Anglo-American landing in western Europe to take the pressure off Russia, still fighting for its life, emerged early in 1942. Some US generals called for a landing in northern France to establish a foothold in 1942, reinforced by a bigger landing in 1943. Churchill urged this very risky plan be dropped in favour of action to clear North Africa and the Mediterranean of Axis troops. Two events – the increased U-boat threat to Atlantic convoys, carrying food and other supplies vital to Britain's continuance in the war, and Rommel's renewed advance into Egypt – delayed even this more modest plan.

Churchill had only reluctantly accepted that the convoy system – pioneered in World War I *after* he had left the Admiralty – offered the one effective way of countering the U-boat menace. This had increased greatly after the fall of France, when the Germans had built bomb-proof U-boat pens in Brest, Brittany. The American merchant navy also proved slow to adopt convoys, and in the first half of 1942 U-boats sank more allied shipping than ever – over 800,000 tons in

March and again in June 1942 – sailing as far south as the unguarded Caribbean. This was more than even the US's booming shipyards could replace, and if continued might by itself have given Hitler victory in the West. But, thanks to improved long-range air patrols using radar, to better protection for convoys and above all to the Ultra deciphering machines at Bletchley in Buckinghamshire, the Battle of the Atlantic was being won by early 1943. The Ultra team, which had begun deciphering German army messages in mid-1940, finally by December 1942 cracked the newest version of the secret Enigma code that the U-boats used and thought indecipherable. Churchill had appreciated the codebreakers' efforts from the start, encouraging them in every way he could, as shown in newly released documents. But the Allies remained desperately short of shipping, which hampered efforts to bring US troops across the Atlantic, especially as the US naval war against Japan meant that the Pacific war, too, needed more ships than it could get.

In Africa, Rommel suddenly renewed his offensive on 28 January 1942, retaking Cyrenaica (Libya). After a pause he captured the important stronghold of Tobruk on 20 June, taking 33,000 prisoners and invaluable fuel supplies. The British were driven back to El Alamein, only 80 miles west of Alexandria, and Egypt seemed threatened. Churchill, again visiting Roosevelt when he got the news, for once let his spirits droop visibly. Roosevelt asked, 'What can we do?' In response, 300 Sherman tanks were shipped east to help the beleaguered 8th Army. However, the Axis advance was checked at the First Battle of El Alamein in July even without them. This defensive victory was not enough for Churchill, however, who had had to face a parliamentary vote of No Confidence in his conduct of the war. He won it by 475 votes to 25, but wanted to see events for himself. Reaching Cairo in August, he urged the army 'to fight and die for victory'. He replaced General Auchinleck with General Alexander as Commander in Chief, with General Bernard Montgomery commanding the 8th Army. Montgomery proved an inspired choice. Churchill's equal in obstinacy and egotism, he carefully built up the 8th Army's morale and fighting strength, refusing to be rushed by Churchill. When he finally attacked on 23 October 1942 in the (second) Battle of El Alamein, Rommel was routed, retreating all the way into Tunisia. This first indisputable land victory was greeted in Britain by the peeling of church bells, silenced since the war started. 'This is not the end', Churchill warned, 'it is not even the beginning of the end. But it is, perhaps, the end of the beginning.' Such sonorous phrases no longer had quite the impact they had in 1940, but he remained personally very popular.

After Egypt, Churchill had gone on to Moscow to meet Stalin in August. Having to tell the Russian dictator that there would be no Second Front that year, was, he later said, 'like carrying a large lump of ice to the North Pole'. Stalin warmed a little when told of Operation Torch, the planned attack on North Africa, and on Churchill's last night they drank together into the small hours. Churchill was repelled but also fascinated by Stalin, who boasted that his forced collectivization of agriculture in the 1930s had killed more Russians than Hitler's armies. But when Stalin called the Allies cowards for not launching the Second Front, Churchill angrily rebuffed him. Despite later attempts to improve relations with 'Uncle Joe' – as the Soviet dictator was known in the West, Russia being seen as heroically fighting Hitler single-handed – Churchill realized that the Soviet Union was not to be fully trusted.

Operation Torch began on 8 November with Anglo-American landings in Morocco and Algeria, both under Vichy French rule. Due to the fortuitous presence in Algeria of Admiral Darlan, a leading Vichyite, French troops surrendered at his orders, but American support for Darlan was an unforgivable snub to General de Gaulle, leader of the Free French. Darland was assassinated soon after. The Germans, far from abandoning Africa, poured fresh troops into Tunisia, and fighting continued until May, with Rommel mauling the Allies at the Kasserine Pass. In January Roosevelt came over to meet Churchill at Casablanca and the two leaders agreed to continue the Mediterranean offensive by invading Sicily and Italy, postponing a landing in France again. They also agreed on German and Japanese 'Unconditional Surrender' – a policy later criticized but intended to ensure that this time Germany accepted its total defeat, as it had not in 1918. After Casablanca Churchill introduced Roosevelt to Marrakech, 'Paris of the Sahara', where he painted a landscape he gave the President. Flying back home in a chilly converted bomber, the 68-year-old Churchill caught pneumonia but with typical resilience soon recovered.

Churchill, if preoccupied with events abroad, did not neglect life in Britain. 'There is no finer investment for any community than putting milk into babies. Healthy citizens are the greatest asset any country can have', he declared in March 1943 and children especially benefited from Britain's remarkably efficient and fair rationing system, which covered clothes and fuel besides food. Even cultural life blossomed, with concerts, plays and a boom in poetry, despite rationing and bombing. The government directed almost every aspect of life in a way inconceivable before the war, which was widely accepted as a wartime necessity. But Labour members of the coalition planned a radical reconstruction of society along socialist lines. Beveridge, Churchill's dynamic civil servant of 30 years before, produced the Beveridge Report in 1942 calling for a national health service, family allowances and full employment – aims about which the government was lukewarm. A Ministry of Reconstruction was set up in 1943 and Education and Town and Country Planning Acts passed in 1944, paving the way for a very different post-war Britain – to the horror of traditional Conservatives. His gaze fixed on the war, Churchill tacitly accepted these social measures, which continued his own youthful reforms.

The capture of Tunis in May with 200,000 Axis prisoners was followed by the invasion of Sicily in July. This led to a coup in Rome that overthrew Mussolini, and the Italians sued for peace in September. Churchill, sensing great if probably unrealizable strategic opportunities in Italy and the Balkans, pressed General Eisenhower, now supreme commander of Allied forces, to ignore Sardinia – 'I absolutely refuse to be fobbed off with a sardine!' – and to strike far up

Italy, so that they could free Rome by Christmas. While the Allies hesitated, the Germans acted, invading Italy *en masse*. Allied landings at Salerno and then Anzio met heavy resistance and Rome was not finally liberated until June 1944. Churchill had his way in one last action: the attempted seizure of Rhodes (formerly Italian occupied) by British forces alone in September 1943. This proved a disastrous failure, however, and Germany's last victory.

The 'Big Three' – Stalin, Roosevelt and Churchill – finally all met at Tehran, Iran, in November 1943. Roosevelt made semi-secret overtures to Stalin which upset Churchill, and took Stalin's claim one evening to have killed 50,000 captive Polish officers (the 'Katyn Massacre') as a joke. Churchill, more perceptive, left the room in protest. The conference ended in mutual toasts – Churchill drank to the International Proletariat, Stalin to the Conservative Party – but no agreement was reached on the fate of post-war Germany.

In the air, Britain had been on the offensive since 1940. Accepting pre-war beliefs in 'precision bombing', the British saw heavy bombers as the one way of hitting back at Germany. Churchill supported this approach, but by November 1941 Professor Lindemann realized that bombing by night – to avoid German fighters – was anything but precise. Instead, a policy of 'area bombing' was adopted, to break German morale by bombing residential areas. In May 1942 the first 1,000-Bomber Raid devastated Cologne. Such raids, reinforced by American daylight attacks, grew steadily in number and size, culminating in the massive bombings of Hamburg, Berlin, Munich and especially Dresden. This last raid on 13 February 1945 killed 130,000 civilians, many refugees, while the railways, the supposed target, were hardly affected. 'Are we beasts?' Churchill cried when watching a film of the devastation, appalled at what he had sanctioned. The bombing offensive finally crippled German industry but at a high cost in both civilian and aircrew deaths – Bomber Command lost over 60,000 airmen, the USAAF even more.

The long-awaited Allied invasion of France, D-day, began on 6 June 1944, with a fleet of 5000 vessels, supported by 7,500 aircraft, which carried almost two million men to Normandy within two months. Churchill, frantic to see the landings himself, had to be personally dissuaded by King George VI, but he visited Normandy on 12 June, just four years after he was last in France. On the return journey the destroyer carrying him fired on enemy-held coast, to his unconcealed delight. Many people that summer hoped, after the liberation of Paris and Rome and the huge Russian advances, the war would soon be over, but Churchill was more cautious, especially after the failure to seize the Rhine bridges at Arnhem in September. He also worried increasingly about growing Soviet power in central Europe, something which most Americans blithely accepted.

Other journeys that year included another transatlantic trip, visits to Italy, where he bathed off Capri, to southern France where he watched the Allied landings there, and to Greece in December, recently liberated. There he committed British troops to supporting the Greek monarchists against the Communists, so triggering a long civil war. (Churchill and Stalin had already privately agreed that in Romania the Soviets would have 90 per cent of the influence, in Greece 90 per cent would be Allied, and in Yugoslavia the division of influence would be 50/50.) Churchill was away from Britain for a total of 20 weeks in 1944, flying around in a special Skymaster plane given him by Roosevelt. Such prolonged absences were surprisingly well accepted by his government.

In February 1945, the Big Three met again at Yalta in the Crimea. Churchill was accommodated in a palatial villa and – despite bed bugs – feasted happily on caviar and Russian champagne, but events did not turn out to his liking. Stalin's troops had already overrun most of eastern and central Europe, and Stalin had his way on issues like Poland's post-war frontiers, moved 200 miles westward, and its future (non-democratic) government. But he promised that Russia would declare war on Japan when Germany was defeated and agreed to proposals for the United Nations, with a Security Council of the US,

Russia, Britain, China and France. (Roosevelt, described by the British Foreign Secretary Eden as 'vague, loose and ineffective' said little. He was actually very ill and died two months later. Churchill, deeply moved, described him as 'the greatest champion of freedom'.) Stalin also agreed to France becoming one of the four 'occupying powers' in Germany but Churchill agreed, rashly, to the repatriation of all 'Russian prisoners' to Russia. This Yalta agreement led to hundreds of thousands of refugees and exiles being returned to their deaths inside the Soviet Union.

The Allies, repelling the German December offensive in the Ardennes, crossed the Rhine in March. Like many Allied generals, Churchill wanted to push for Berlin, the German capital, but Eisenhower held all Allied armies back, letting the Russians capture the city instead. On 7 May 1945, the Germans unconditionally surrendered and VE day, 'Victory in Europe' was announced. Churchill appeared on the balcony of Buckingham Palace with the royal family to tumultuous acclaim from the crowds below. It did not save him from crushing, unexpected electoral defeat only two months later. Despite Churchill's personal popularity, the British people wanted a change of government and Labour, perhaps helped by his unwise talk of Labour needing 'a Gestapo' to implement its policies, won a huge majority. Suddenly, after nearly six years' frantic work, Churchill was out of office.

Elder Statesman 11

Like most people in Britain, Churchill was stunned by Labour's unexpectedly massive victory – it won 393 seats to the Conservatives' 189. Clementine, aware of her husband's underlying exhaustion, called it a blessing in disguise, but he was little comforted. However, although he decided to remain as leader of the Conservatives – rather than 'retiring gracefully in an odour of civic freedoms' – he now had time to take far lengthier trips abroad. He spent the late summer in a villa on Lake Como, Italy, lent by General Alexander, painting and swimming. Early in 1946 he visited the US as a guest of President Truman where he gave a prophetic warning in Fulton, Missouri, about the rapid but enforced spread of Soviet Communism. 'From Stettin in the Baltic to Trieste in the Adriatic, an iron curtain has descended across the Continent', he declared. 'Behind that line ... police governments are prevailing in nearly every case.' This first use of the term 'iron curtain', was perceptive at a time when many still hoped Stalin would participate positively in post-war reconstruction. Not everyone welcomed it even in the US, some Congressmen hankering after a return to pre-war isolationism.

Back in Europe, he called for improved Franco-German relations as the essential basis for post-war Europe. Such recognition of Germany's central role in post-war Europe was unusual – though typical of Churchill's magnanimity to the conquered – just when the full horrors of the Reich were being revealed at the Nuremberg War Crimes Tribunal. In January 1947, at a 'United Europe Meeting' in the Albert Hall in London, Churchill spoke of the four 'main pillars of the World Temple of Peace' – the US, the British Empire, the Soviet Union and lastly Europe 'with which Great Britain is profoundly blended'. That summer 'Marshall Aid' was inaugurated, an American economic programme that vastly helped all western Europe, including Britain.

At the Hague, Holland, in May 1948, attending the founding of the United Europe Campaign, Churchill received a standing ovation that moved him to tears. But he remained ambiguous about whether Britain should join a new united Europe or merely encourage it. In 1950 he declared that British 'national sovereignty is not inviolable' vis-à-vis Europe, but in practice he never committed Britain to anything. In his travels round Europe and the US, complete with cases of champagne, he was now treated like royalty and showered with honours.

The growth in West European unity was partly a response to threatening Soviet actions in Eastern Europe. In March 1948, the Communists snuffed out democracy in Czechoslovakia and in June the Russians cut Berlin's land links to the West, hoping to starve out the western part of the divided city and so take it over. The Allies responded with the Berlin Airlift, a remarkable demonstration of airpower that saved West Berlin. NATO, the North Atlantic Treaty Organisation, was established in April 1949, binding the US, most West European countries and Britain in a defensive alliance. In all these matters, Labour policies were much the same as the Conservatives', which made the Opposition's task harder. Only over India was there a true difference of opinion. The Attlee government accepted the need for speedy independence and reluctantly accepted partition along religious lines in India and Pakistan as Mountbatten, the last Viceroy, suggested. Churchill was grieved by 'the clattering down of the British Empire with all its glories' and the bloodshed accompanying independence in August 1947 exceeded his gloomiest prophecies. But even here he was not speaking for all Conservatives, for Halifax gave independence a qualified welcome. Despite initially dismissing Nehru, the first Indian Prime Minister, as a 'man of straw', Churchill too accepted Indian independence with surprising swiftness, even inviting Nehru to dinner when in London in 1950. He warmly welcomed the establishment of the state of Israel in 1948, however, seeing it as fulfilling his earlier ideas.

At times Churchill was criticized by his own party for his frequent absences from the House of Commons, and there were even occasional rumours of a plot to replace him. But no one else could rival him when on form, certainly not Anthony Eden, his 'crown prince' or successor. As Beaverbrook remarked: 'When Mr Churchill is in his seat, the Opposition breathes fire. When he is not, the Tory front bench has all the venom of a bunch of daffodils.' A major problem for the Tories was how far to accept Labour's radical social reforms, in many cases actually conceived by the wartime coalition. 'Rab' Butler, appointed by Churchill to head the Research Department, produced in 1947 an Industrial Charter that accepted the nationalization of the Bank of England and the coal mines – to the wrath of many right-wingers – but opposed nationalizing the steel industry. In 1949 Churchill personally corrected Butler's document *The Right Road for Britain*, which outlined the moderate Conservatism later termed 'Butskellism', prevalent until 1975. There was more scope for criticizing the excessive regulations of every aspect of life and the continuing grim rationing.

During this period, Churchill was much occupied with his *History of the Second World War*, whose sales – volume 1 alone sold 221,000 in Britain, 75,000 in the US – made him a rich man. He bought two London houses at Hyde Park Gate – one as a home, one as an office – while reopening Chartwell, which had been bought by the National Trust but given to him for his life. He stocked the grounds with exotic birds and animals and enjoyed playing the country squire again, although his farming never paid. However, he also bought a race horse, Colonist II, which won him £11,938 in prizes. In general, his appetite for life was undiminished. At one lunch he gave for members of his shadow cabinet he ate a dozen oysters, two helpings of roast beef and apple pie with ice cream, along with wine and brandy. He even still hunted and swam. In August 1949, while holidaying at Beaverbrook's villa on the French Riviera, he stayed up drinking and playing cards until the small hours. He then suffered a small stroke, but recovered swiftly once more. 'The dagger struck', he said later, 'but this time it was not plunged into the hilt'. Death never seemed to worry him. 'I am prepared to meet my Maker. Whether my Maker is prepared for the great ordeal of meeting me is another matter', he joked in 1954.

Meanwhile, he carried on rallying the Conservatives and harrying a Labour government now looking increasingly tired. In January 1950, Attlee called a General Election. Churchill, on holiday in Madeira, at once flew back by flying-boat. He personally campaigned more vigorously around the country than in 1945 but Labour won again, though with a majority of only eight. If the middle classes had swung back to the Conservatives, the working classes were still solidly Labour. Another early election was postponed by the outbreak of the Korean War, in which British troops fought alongside Americans against the invading Chinese Communists. The war's chief effect was to increase the inflation rate – because of higher global demand for raw materials – and so help the Conservatives win the General Election of October 1951, but with a majority of only 17. Typically, Churchill tried to get the Liberals to join his government, without success.

Churchill was now 77 and, if generally fit for a man of his age, looked unlikely to remain Prime Minister for long. He spoke of retiring after about a year, but circumstances, combined with his reluctance to leave office, kept him in power for far longer. Churchill appointed familiar faces to his Cabinet – Eden became Foreign Secretary, Butler Chancellor of the Exchequer, Lord Alexander Defence Secretary, Macmillan Minister of Housing – arousing indignation from newer MPs who were overlooked. Economic problems at first predominated; a balance of payments crisis required an increase in bank rate and curbs on imports as Britain struggled to combine massive expenditure on defence and social programmes. The government was determined to honour its election pledges of building 300,000 new houses a year – Churchill's own slogan for the election had been 'Houses, red meat and not getting scuppered'. It could not at once, however, end meat rationing as promised. (Churchill, when a typical ration of meat, bread and sugar was produced for him on a plate, murmured, 'Not a bad meal, not a bad meal.' He was shocked to discover this was meant to last an ordinary person a whole week.)

King George VI died suddenly of lung cancer in February 1952. Churchill, deeply moved, spoke with majestic eloquence: 'During these last months the King walked with death as if death were a companion, an acquaintance … In the end, death came as a friend … I, whose youth was passed in the august, unchallenged and tranquil glories of the Victorian era may well feel a thrill in invoking once more the prayer and Anthem, "God Save the Queen".' The new queen, Elizabeth II, flying back from an official tour of Africa, was greeted at the airport by Churchill, who developed an avuncular yet romantic devotion to her recalling that of Lord Melbourne and the young Queen Victoria. He accepted a Knighthood of the Garter and organized the elaborate Coronation in Westminster Abbey – the first ever televised – in June 1953. There was talk of a New Elizabethan Age, boosted by the coincidental first ascent of Mt Everest by Edmund Hilary, news of which actually reached Britain on Coronation Day.

Just three weeks later, on 23 June, Churchill suffered his third and worst stroke, whose seriousness only gradually became apparent. He had been very busy that year, running the Foreign Office as well as arranging the Coronation, for Eden had had a series of operations. Paradoxically, this meant that, with his designated successor disabled, Churchill could carry on as Prime Minister, recuperating out of sight – attended by a faithful but soon exhausted Clementine – while Rab Butler effectively headed the government, chairing Cabinet meetings. This highly irregular situation lasted through the summer, for Churchill's stroke was kept secret. He went on holiday to Beaverbrook's Riviera villa as normal in August, although he could not lift his arm even to paint. But by October he was well enough to give a rousing speech at the Party Conference at Margate: 'If I stay on for the time being bearing the burden at my age, it is not because of love for power or office. I have had an ample share of both. If I stay, it is because I have a feeling that I may … have an influence on what I care about above all else, the building of a sure and lasting peace.' The cheers that greeted this speech helped persuade him to stay on.

Churchill's chief concerns in these last years in office were indeed world peace and the dangers posed by the new hydrogen bomb. He supported the armistice ending the Korean War in 1953 and cut general defence spending. But, wanting as ever to negotiate from a position of strength, he supported the development of a separate British nuclear deterrent in 1952, for the Americans in 1946 had abruptly ended the partnership of Britain, Canada and the US that had produced the first atom bomb. After Stalin's death in March 1953, he saw possibilities of a rapprochement with the new Soviet leadership under Malenkov. Sailing over with a huge entourage on the liner *Queen Elizabeth*, he tried to persuade Eisenhower, the new American president, of the need for a world summit meeting, but without success.

Some issues did not attract him, such as the proposed European Defence Community (EDC) which at the time seemed vital for West European liberty and the European Coal and Steel Community, established in 1952, the forerunner of the present EU. For missing these opportunities he was later criticized, but Churchill was in tune with current British opinion, not yet ready even to contemplate joining Europe. The Empire, apart from the loss of India, still appeared as large if not quite as glorious as ever. He also declined to do battle with the trade unions, preferring to compromise over pay disputes, so sowing the seeds of many later inflationary problems. Butler said that Churchill was 'brave in war but cowardly in peace', but he was now an old man. On 30 November 1954, his eightieth birthday was celebrated with two birthday cakes from both Houses of Parliament and a presentation of a portrait by Graham Sutherland, one of the finest living portraitists. Churchill publicly accepted it as 'a remarkable example of modern art … it combines force with grandeur' but privately detested it, saying it made him look malignant and sottish. After his death, Clementine destroyed it, but photographs suggest an image of aged, decaying grandeur.

Churchill's retirement could no longer be deferred. On 5 April 1955, he finally announced it – after a grand dinner party at No 10. He declined the offer of a dukedom from the Queen, as his son Randolph still harboured political ambitions – always frustrated because he never won a seat. Eden succeeded as Prime Minister and at once called a General Election, which the Conservatives won with an increased majority. But Churchill, though he comfortably retained his own seat, now took very little part in political life, partly because he was now very deaf. After all the years of immense energy and ambition, he had nothing left to live for, instead filling his days with reading novels, painting, playing cards and travelling to his favourite sun spots, principally Marrakech and the Riviera. Only the completion of his *History of the English-Speaking Peoples* – which lovingly described every battle but did not mention Shakespeare once – occupied a mind now sinking at times into depression and somnolence. Old friends died – some, like Brendan Bracken, not so old at only 57 – and although he made new friends such as the Greek billionaire Aristotle Onassis, who took him for long relaxing cruises on his yacht, he felt increasingly isolated. A series of minor strokes, falls with accompanying fractures and attacks of pneumonia gradually wore him down, although he still enjoyed his food, cognac and cigars. He celebrated his ninetieth birthday with a family party but on 9 January 1965 he refused his cigars and cognac, lying in bed immobile. Another stroke was diagnosed, a great crowd gathered outside his house in Hyde Park Gate and finally, on 24 January 1965, he died. More than 320,000 people filed past his coffin as it lay in state at Westminster Hall. Flags flew at half-mast. The state funeral – the first for a subject since the funeral of the Duke of Wellington in 1852 – was attended by many heads of state, including his old ally and rival General de Gaulle, and televised around the world. At its end, his coffin was taken by boat and steam train – named *The Winston Churchill* – to Bladon, near Blenheim, where he was buried next to his ancestors.

Churchill is often called 'the greatest Englishman of the century'. Certainly no British politician since has been able to dominate the global stage, nor inspire and unite his countrymen as Churchill did in 1940, so saving not just the British Empire (for a while) but also all European civilization from the most odious tyranny that has ever threatened it. For all his numerous faults, both personal and political, Churchill at his finest and bravest appealed to the finest and bravest in others, but he himself retained, beneath his grand rhetoric, an irreverent sense of humour and a warm humanity, even sentimentality, that made him unique.

FURTHER READING

Books by Churchill on his own life and career

The World Crisis (5 vols, 1923–31)

My Early Life, London (1930)

The Second World War (6 vols, 1948–54)

A History of the English-Speaking Peoples (4 vols, 1956–58)

Books about Churchill

Blake, Robert and William Louis (ed.) *Churchill* (1933)

Bonham Carter, Violet *Winston Churchill as I Knew Him* (1965)

Brendon, Piers *Winston Churchill: A Brief Life* (1984)

Gilber, Martin *Winston S Churchill* (1971)

James, Rhodes *Churchill, A Study in Failure* (1900–39)

Lamb, Richard *Churchill as War Leader* (1991)

Pelling, Henry *Winston Churchill* (1974)

Talor, A.J.P. et al *Churchill: Four Faces and the Man* (1969)

INDEX

FREUD – A BEGINNER'S GUIDE

Ruth Berry

Freud – A Beginner's Guide introduces you to the 'father of psychoanalysis' and his work. No need to wrestle with difficult concepts as key ideas are presented in a clear and jargon-free way.

Ruth Berry's informative text explores:

- Freud's background and the times he lived in
- the development of psychoanalysis
- the ideas surrounding Freud's work on the unconscious.

The facts … the concepts … the ideas …

ISAAC NEWTON – A BEGINNER'S GUIDE

Jane Jakeman

Isaac Newton – A Beginner's Guide introduces you to this 17th century genius. Explore how his scientific discoveries revolutionized our world and his philosophy changed our thought. Learn about Newton the scientist, philosopher, alchemist and respected public figure.

Jane Jakeman's lively text:

- describes Newton's background and the times he lived in
- explores his scientific ideas and their effect on our lives
- delves into the character of this great man
- examines the influence of Newton both in his own time and today.

The facts … the concepts … the ideas …

GANDHI – A BEGINNER'S GUIDE

Genevieve Blais

Gandhi – A Beginner's Guide invites you to take a glimpse into the life of this profound character. Follow his extraordinary quest for morality, justice and spirituality and discover how his strategy of passive resistance achieved social reform.

Genevieve Blais's compelling text investigates:

- Gandhi's background and the times he lived in
- Britain's role in the history of India
- the events leading up to and prior to the Salt March
- Gandhi's role in the independence of India, his assassination and legacy.

The facts … the concepts … the ideas …

HITLER – A BEGINNER'S GUIDE

Nigel Rodgers

Hitler – A Beginner's Guide inspires you to discover what makes this most monstrous of modern tyrants so uniquely fascinating. Discover how the young Hitler was an utter failure and follow his rise to supreme power in the chaos of Weimar Germany.

Nigel Rodgers' vivid text explores:

- Hitler's background and the times he lived in
- the hidden forces behind Hitler's meteoric career
- Hitler's powers as a spellbinding orator
- Hitler's belief in war and how this brought his subsequent downfall
- the final solution.

The facts … the concepts … the ideas …